THE DOUBLE-JACK MURDERS

This Large Print Book carries the
Seal of Approval of N.A.V.H.

A SHERIFF BO TULLY MYSTERY

THE DOUBLE-JACK MURDERS

PATRICK F. MCMANUS

THORNDIKE PRESS
A part of Gale, Cengage Learning

Detroit • New York • San Francisco • New Haven, Conn • Waterville, Maine • London

GALE
CENGAGE Learning™

Copyright © 2009 by Patrick F. McManus.
Thorndike Press, a part of Gale, Cengage Learning.

Thorndike Press® Large Print Mystery.
The text of this Large Print edition is unabridged.
Other aspects of the book may vary from the original edition.
Set in 16 pt. Plantin.
Printed on permanent paper.

LIBRARY OF CONGRESS CATALOGING-IN-PUBLICATION DATA

McManus, Patrick F.
   The double-jack murders : a sheriff Bo Tully mystery / by
Patrick F. McManus.
     p. cm. — (Thorndike Press large print mystery)
   ISBN-13: 978-1-4104-2297-2 (alk. paper)
   ISBN-10: 1-4104-2297-6 (alk. paper)
   1. Sheriffs—Idaho—Fiction. 2. Idaho—Fiction. 3. Large type
books. I. Title.
PS3563.C38625D68 2010
813'.54—dc22
                                          2009041317

Published in 2010 by arrangement with Simon & Schuster, Inc.

To my four excellent daughters:
Kelly, Shannon, Peggy, and Erin

1

Idaho's Blight County sheriff, Bo Tully, scanned the ridge above his log house with binoculars. Nothing. Still too dark to make out anything beyond the tree line. He sighed, letting the binoculars dangle down his chest. Behind him on the porch, a little brown-and-white dog perched on a padded bar stool. The dog watched the sheriff intently, as if sensing some danger.

Tully glanced at the dog. "Still too dark to see anything, Clarence. You don't have to worry, anyway. It's me he's after, not you."

Clarence laid his chin down on his paws.

"Sure," Tully said to him. "*Now* you relax!"

The sun began to rise over the ridge to the east. Soon its rays penetrated the tree line on the west ridge. Tully, wearing khakis, a red-and-blue tattersall shirt, a well-aged leather jacket, and his three-thousand-dollar alligator-skin cowboy boots, raised the binoculars and again scanned the woods. A deer stood there, gazing down at the meadow. A good sign. Tully could detect no movement among the trees. He turned at the sound of a motor. A pickup truck was coming down the road that wound across the meadow to his house. Deputy Brian Pugh pulled up and got out of the truck. He was wearing jeans, a sweatshirt, and a baseball cap. He was ridiculously trim and fit. His squinty eyes gave his face a hard look, softened a bit by the brown mustache that adorned his upper lip. A sheriff's department badge was fastened to a pocket of his faded jeans.

"Morning, Bo."

"Morning, Pugh."

The dog raised his head off his paws and growled.

"Shut up, Clarence," Pugh said as he came up the porch steps. "I don't like criminals growling at me." He was referring to the little dog's several arrests for hiding under cars and biting people on the ankles, usually a little old lady with an armload of packages. Clarence stopped growling.

Tully said, "You wouldn't like a nice little dog, would you, Pugh?"

"No way. You were supposed to take Clarence out in the woods and knock him off. It's not my fault you're turning soft."

"Don't let it get around. Anyway, I've got a place all fixed up for you by the window in the studio upstairs. The rifle is sighted in at three hundred yards. That should give you a dead-on shot."

"How can I be sure it's Kincaid?"

"I've got a major spotting scope up there. At three hundred yards, you should be able to pick out the sex of a mosquito on his face. I suspect he may be wearing that stupid cap of his, the red-and-black-plaid one with the earflaps tied up on top. Besides, he'll have a rifle with him. Shouldn't be anybody up there with a rifle in June."

"You want me to kill him, right?" Pugh said.

Tully gave him his crooked smile, a look known to the members of his department as The Look.

"Gotcha."

Tully got up and opened the door for Pugh. "As you know, I've got company coming today — lots of it. So don't be poking the rifle barrel out the window. No point in making folks nervous. I fixed you up a comfortable chair and a good rest for the rifle. I guess you know your way up to the studio."

"Yup."

"One other thing, Pugh."

9

"What's that?"

"Don't miss."

Pugh went inside just as a large flatbed truck came lumbering down the road. The bed of the truck was piled high with green picnic tables and benches. They had been collected from the city park by two of the sheriff's deputies. The truck stopped three-quarters of the way down the road. Men got out and began unloading the tables and benches and arranging them about the meadow. They had done all this before. Shortly thereafter, pickup trucks began arriving with coolers stacked in the beds, the wild-game contents of his deputies' freezers. This was the fourth annual Sheriff Bo Tully Empty the Freezer Day, one of the greatest political ploys ever committed in the entire history of Blight County, perhaps even in the history of Idaho or even of the United States. Tully couldn't help but smile.

A couple hours later, cars began turning off the highway and parking in the upper part of the meadow. The occupants got out and came down the road carrying shovels and axes. They began digging holes in the sod of the meadow and lining the holes with rocks. Some of the men carried firewood and piled it next to the holes. Soon a dozen fires were burning in the meadow, an area

Tully usually referred to as his yard. Iron racks were set up next to some of the fires, while others were fitted out with grills.

By noon, slabs of deer and elk ribs were roasting on the iron racks. Grills simmered with smoked elk sausages, elk and venison steaks, and various kinds of ground meat patties — deer, elk, bear, moose, antelope, sheep, porcupine, and enough mystery meats to cover most of the other wild animal species of Idaho. Tully had once tried what turned out to be a weasel patty and from then on had taken care to avoid all mystery meats.

One large bed of coals contained foil-wrapped packages of sliced potatoes and onions. Huge skillets of grouse gravy bubbled on two charcoal grills. Smoked kokanee salmon protruded in pink and golden patinas out of greasy boxes. Tables were laden with double rows of salads — potato, pasta, Jell-O, carrot-raisin, coleslaw, ambrosia, layered, sauerkraut, four-bean, and fruit. All of the salads had been provided by residents of Blight County, along with enough pies to cover the tops of several tables. Assorted local bands took turns furnishing the musical background.

By one o'clock Sheriff Bo Tully's Freezer Day was in full gluttonous uproar. Local

11

politicians and their spouses filled two tables that had been pushed together. They glanced enviously around at the partying crowd. Why hadn't one of them thought of this scam?

Tully smiled. Absently scratching an itch through his shirt, he made a rough calculation of the number of votes represented in his yard and meadow, more than enough, he calculated, to guarantee his winning the next election hands-down, in the unlikely event he even had an opponent. The citizens of Blight County loved him, particularly the women. His close scrutiny of the crowd, however, had little to do with votes. His interest lay in one Lucas Kincaid, a nasty piece of work if ever there was one.

After serving only two months of a life sentence for murder and the cultivation and sale of marijuana, Kincaid had somehow escaped from a prison van hauling him to a hospital for a mental evaluation that Tully himself could have provided — crazy! Kincaid had left the two guards accompanying him dead, not because of any necessity related to his escape but, Tully mused, probably as an afterthought. The homicidal maniac had soon let it be known about the county that his first order of business was to kill the man who had put him in prison, one Sheriff Bo Tully. Some people are such sore losers.

Tully's eyes fixed on a figure advancing toward him through the crowd. It was a very nice figure. The pretty blond woman wore a white dress distinguished mostly for its brevity, one of Tully's favorite elements of female fashion. Coming up to the porch, she held out her hand. Tully leaped to his feet, grasped the hand, and gave it a little squeeze.

The young woman laughed. "You are even more handsome than my aunt let on," she said, her blue eyes twinkling.

"How is that possible?" Tully said. "And exactly who is this extraordinarily perceptive aunt? More to the point, who are you, sweetheart?"

She tried to pull back her hand but Tully refused to let it go. In such cases, he didn't believe in catch-and-release.

"Bunny Hunter," she said, laughing. "My aunt is Agatha Wrenn. Actually, she is my great-aunt."

Tully dropped her hand. "Agatha! Agatha sent her young and beautiful niece to see me? She must be in the grip of Alzheimer's."

"Not at all," Bunny said, smiling as she unstuck a wisp of blond hair from her perspiring face. "Her mind is very sharp,

13

even the more so for someone up in her eighties. In fact before sending me on this mission, she warned me extensively about you. So I am well prepared to fend off your charms, should you attempt to display any."

"And here I thought I already had," Tully said. "My supply of charms must be running low today. So what can I do for you, Miss Hunter? Or, rather, for your Aunt Agatha? She and her friend Bernice, by the way, just happen to be two of my most favorite people in the entire world." He sat down on a porch step and motioned for Bunny to sit down beside him. "Please have a step, Miss Hunter."

"Thanks," she said, sitting down and demurely smoothing her dress, which reached almost halfway to her dimpled knees.

"Now tell me," Tully said, "exactly what is the mission Aunt Agatha has sent you on?"

"I'm to persuade you to solve a mystery for her."

"My specialty!"

Bunny laughed. "This one is really weird, though. I'm embarrassed even to bring it up but I promised I would. She wants you to find out if her father — my great-grandfather — was murdered and, if so, by whom."

"I see. And what makes Agatha think her

father may have been murdered?"

At that moment a pixyish little man strode by, his hat pulled down onto his ears, his hands thrust deep into his pockets.

"Petey!" Tully roared.

The little man jumped and spun around. "Bo! You scared me half to death!"

"I thought I had you in jail, Petey!"

"You did, Bo! I got sprung yesterday!"

"Oh? Well, in that case, have a good time. Stop by the pie table. My mom's ramrodding it. Tell her I said to give you something special."

"I'll tell her you said so, Bo." Petey went on his way.

"Sorry about that," he said to Bunny, who wore a startled expression. "I have a hard time keeping track of my criminals."

"I can see that." She went on to answer his question. "Agatha's father disappeared one day back in 1927. His helper, Sean O'Boyle, a boy of about fourteen, disappeared with him. One day they went off to work a small gold mine they had hidden away in the Snowy Mountains and were never seen nor heard from again. Agatha claims her mother told her that her father wasn't the kind of man to run off like that. All these years, Agatha has wondered what happened to the two of them. She believes they must have been murdered or maybe killed in a mine cave-in. Agatha says you can figure out if they were murdered and, if so, who did it. She thinks you're a genius."

"Really? Well, she has always been extraordinarily perceptive. I became aware of it when I was one of her students at the U. of I. Oddly, I don't recall she thought I was a genius back in those days."

"She does now. Anyway, may I tell Aunt Agatha you will look into the mystery? I realize there's no chance you could solve a crime that old, even if there was one, but maybe you could at least pretend to, for Agatha's sake."

"Pretend! You've got to be kidding, Miss Hunter. Of course I'll come up and solve the mystery. As it happens I've been thinking of taking a vacation and getting out of town for a while. Solving this little puzzle sounds like just the kind of vacation I most enjoy. Are you by any chance hanging out at the ranch?"

Bunny laughed. "Why, yes I am. I'm staying there for the summer to work on the dissertation for my doctorate in American studies at Washington State University."

"Wonderful!" Tully said. "You couldn't have a better mentor around than Agatha."

"That's for sure. Well, I hope you'll stop

by the ranch soon."

"You can count on it."

Bunny gave Tully a blazing smile, stood up, and dusted off the seat of her tiny dress, a gesture that caused Tully's heart to skip two beats. She disappeared into the crowd of picnickers.

Yes, Tully thought, he would definitely make a point of driving up to Quail Creek Ranch. Might even work up a scheme to kill two birds with one stone. Well, maybe three birds, counting Bunny.

A trim, elderly man with close-cropped white hair walked out onto the porch. He carried a steaming plate of shrimp. "Who's the babe?"

"None of your business," Tully said. "You're much too old to be eyeing a woman like that. Could bring on a heart attack."

"I did feel a twinge when she brushed off her seat," Pap Tully said.

"Not a bad way to go, though."

Tully smiled at his father. "Never ends, does it?"

"Nope, it don't."

"So where did the shrimp come from? They smell wonderful!"

"Anything does, cooked in butter and garlic. There's a guy in your kitchen cooking up huge piles of them."

"Really? I better pay this mystery chef a visit."

"He seems to have about a ton of shrimp. Said his seafood truck broke down outside of Blight, so he figured he might as well bring the shrimp over for your Freezer Day. Saw one of your posters on a utility pole. Man, I wish I'd have had enough sense to come up with this scam when I was sheriff."

Tully chuckled. "I reckon this was the only scam you missed." He walked into the house and picked up a plate from a stack on his living-room table. A man in Tully's "Wild in the Kitchen" camouflage apron was at his range, scooping heaps of shrimp onto the plate of a plump young woman. "They smell divine!" she said.

Tully stepped up and held out his plate. "Nice apron."

"Thanks. I found it in that closet over there."

"Where did you come from anyway?"

The mystery chef looked up from his skillet. His gray hair was longish but trimmed in an expensive cut. Wire-rimmed glasses sat low on his nose, which glistened with sweat. "And you are?"

"I'm the guy who owns the kitchen."

"Ah, the famous Bo Tully, sheriff and artist. I'm Sid Brown, owner of the Giggling

Loon Restaurant in Boise." He held out his hand. Tully shook it. "You have a very nice kitchen here, Sheriff. And please don't view my intrusion as an intrusion."

"Not at all, Sid. In fact, your shrimp appear to be the highlight of my Freezer Day. I hope your truck breaks down every time you haul shrimp through Blight."

"Actually, I had another truck come up from Boise to haul out the halibut and salmon. I decided to hold back the shrimp, though, after I saw a poster about your Freezer Day. I've been a big fan of your painting for years."

"Really?"

"Yes, indeed. I have four of your watercolors hanging in my restaurant and two more on the walls at home."

"Six of my watercolors! You're obviously rich."

"I am rich, but I got your watercolors back when they were still cheap."

Tully smiled and sampled a shrimp. "They sold a lot better when they were cheap. Sid, these shrimp are delicious. You can come to my Freezer Day anytime."

"You're a terrific artist, Bo. I bought all the paintings from Jean Runyan's gallery in Spokane. Jean's been talking you up for years. Wants to put on a one-man show for you."

"It's a pretty small gallery, but I would love a show."

"She says she would try to put it in the mezzanine of the Davenport Hotel."

"Wow, the Davenport. That's pretty classy."

"You bet it's classy. And she wants the loan of my paintings along with whatever you have or can collect."

Tully held out his plate for shrimp. Sid heaped it full. Tully picked up one and ate it. He smacked his lips. "You're definitely an artist with shrimp, Sid."

"I love any kind of art. I had it all to do over again, I'd try to be an artist. I think being an artist is the best kind of life there is."

"Yeah, it beats chasing criminals, I can tell you that. Right now I've got a criminal chasing me, which is even worse."

"I heard about that homicidal maniac," Sid said. "I guess just about everyone around here has." He pointed at a painting on Tully's living-room wall. "Say, I don't suppose you'd sell me that big oil of the girl coming through the door with a bouquet of wildflowers."

Tully turned and looked at the painting.

20

"Naw, afraid not. That's my wife."

"She's beautiful. I'd love to meet her. I had no idea you were married."

"Yeah, that's kind of a problem. I have the feeling I'm still married to Ginger, but she died ten years ago. Foolish, huh?"

"I don't know. I kind of like the idea."

"Don't get me wrong," Tully said. "I still date other women."

"That's what I hear."

"No doubt. Everybody hears that. It's mostly because of my mother. She's Gossip Central in Blight City. Anyway, I did that painting of Ginger just a couple of years ago. Did it from memory. I retained the image of Ginger coming through the door with the bouquet of wildflowers all that time, right down to the last detail."

He picked up another plate and asked Sid to fill it with shrimp. "I got kind of an invalid up in the studio. I better take him up some shrimp, before he starts raising a fuss."

Deputy Brian Pugh was sweeping the spotting scope back and forth, studying the tree line on top of the ridge.

"Heard me coming up the stairs, huh, Pugh?"

"You know me, Bo, nothing if not vigilant. I was starting to wonder when you might

21

get up here with some of that shrimp. The aroma has been driving me crazy." He picked up a shrimp by the tail, munched it, and then moaned with pleasure. "You can have me watch your back anytime."

"I plan to," Tully said. "I don't suppose you've put the scope on any pretty ladies."

"Like a blonde in a tiny white dress? No, sir, I've been focused entirely on bad guys with rifles sneaking through the woods."

"Yeah, right. Speaking of bad guys, I don't like the idea of being used as bait for Lucas Kincaid."

"Hey, it was your idea, Bo."

"Yeah. Not one of my better ones though. I'm a sitting duck here in town. I think we'd better move our operation to the mountains."

"You're the boss. But the mountains are home for Kincaid. I think he will be a lot tougher to nail up there."

"Yeah, well, you'll be happy to know that I'm going to take off a week and go camping up north with Pap." He studied his deputy's face. "Your expression tells me you think I'm afraid of Lucas Kincaid. Listen, Brian, I've had a lot smarter men than Lucas try to kill me and they're all either dead or in prison. So I don't want you or any of the other deputies to think I'm running off because of Kincaid."

"How about a tiny white dress?"

"That's a different matter."

Pugh stretched and yawned. He turned and stared up at the tree line. "I don't suppose you want to let me know where you're camping?"

"I was going to bring that up. It's that old campsite on Deadman Creek. You know the one. There used to be horse-packing operations out of there, and part of the old corral is still standing."

"That the one with a ridge above it?"

"Yeah, you can see the ridge from the camp and the camp from the ridge. Otherwise the trees are pretty thick around it. It's terrific deer hunting, but you have to be able to shoot quick. I nailed a deer up on the ridge from the camp, though. Good elk hunting, too. There's some clear country higher up and lots of times you can even get a rest for a long shot."

"I'll give it a try sometime."

"Do that."

Tully returned to the porch to find his bulky deputy Buck Toole talking to the local Catholic priest, Father James Flynn, who was sitting in Tully's rocker. Clarence was baring his teeth at the priest. "Make yourself at home, Flynn," Tully said. "And don't mind Clarence. He's a Protestant."

"You showed up just in time, Bo," the priest said. "I made the mistake of complimenting Buck on his scars, and I think he's about to take off his shirt to show me some more."

Two years before, Buck had spent several weeks in the hospital recovering from gunshot wounds. Tully was fairly sure the shots had been meant for him, not Buck. They both had been driving red sheriff's department Ford Explorers. He said, "Forget the body scars, Buck. The only worthwhile scars are those on your face, and you have a couple of nice ones. Make him far handsomer than he was before, don't you think, Flynn?"

"That's hard to imagine."

"I know. He's still ugly as sin but at least the scars give him some character."

"Thanks," the deputy said. "It's nice to be appreciated."

Pap strolled up. "I've got a lot more impressive scars than Buck." He started to unbutton his shirt.

Tully said, "I just explained scars don't amount to much if you've got to unbutton your shirt every time you want to show them off. What happened, Padre — this was back in the sixties — three bad guys were

24

holed up behind a pile of logs. The other law-enforcement guys were using common sense and waiting them out. Pap showed up, walked over the log pile, and killed all three of them with a pump shotgun, but not before they put a few bullets in him. He later got a medal from the governor for stupidity beyond the call of reason."

"Heroism!" Pap corrected. After pointing out the little pucker marks from the bullets, he buttoned his shirt back up.

"Very impressive," the priest said.

"Don't encourage him, Flynn," Tully said. "By the way, you make a contribution to my Freezer Day?"

"You bet. The toughest elk meat ever visited upon the folks of Blight County."

"I told you not to shoot, but would you listen? No."

"I never listen to a heathen when it comes to shooting the biggest elk I've ever seen," the priest said. "Speaking of hunting, I hope your friends are taking good care of the birds on their ranch."

"I assume you are talking about Quail Creek Ranch. You're just lucky, Flynn, that you get to associate with a person dearly beloved by the owners of that property. As a matter of fact, they put in a new guzzler for the birds up in the high country."

"Guzzler?" said the priest. "What's a guzzler?"

"It's a big tub-like thing that catches rainwater and stores it for the birds. Guzzlers are one reason Quail Creek Ranch provides fantastic bird hunting over several thousand acres. They've got three or four scattered around."

"The quail have a creek to drink from."

"Not in the high country. It's very dry up where the chukars hang out."

"Those are two of the orneriest old women in the country," Pap said. "But they do love Bo."

"Hey, don't talk about my friends that way," Tully said.

"It's just that all the ladies love Bo," Pap said.

"You still dating the medical examiner?" Flynn asked.

"On-again, off-again."

"I ain't touching that one," Buck said.

"Me, neither," said Pap. "Not with the padre sitting here."

Tully chose not to mention that Susan Parker had tired of him and taken up with an airline pilot.

Just then a freckled kid in bib overalls came by. He was gnawing on a rib. He stopped and looked at Clarence. "That your

26

dog, Bo?"

"I guess."

"Can I pet him?"

"If you want to, Richy. Matter of fact, I'll give him to you."

Richy walked up on the porch and over to Clarence. "Dang! He tried to bite me, Bo! I don't want no dog that bites!"

"I figured you might be picky," Tully said. "If you know some fellows don't mind a minor flaw in a dog, send them over to me, okay, Richy?"

The kid stomped off.

Tully stretched and yawned. "Well, it's getting to be a long day, guys. I better let you folks hold down the porch here, while I stop by the office and wake up my skeleton crew. Buck, I got Pugh up in the studio, probably napping. Tell him he might as well go home."

"I bet you got him on the lookout for Kincaid," Buck said. "Shucks, old Lucas would be crazy, try to kill you."

"He *is* crazy, Buck."

2

Tully savored the sound his three-thousand-dollar alligator-skin boots made on the marble-chip floor of the courthouse — *clok, clok, clok, clok*. Any kind of cowboy boots would make a similar sound, but there was something expensive about the *clok* of these boots. The money had come from the sale of his latest watercolor, and that, too, made the boots special. He was getting closer every day to becoming a full-time artist. It couldn't be soon enough.

"Everybody snap to!" he shouted as he walked into the sheriff's department briefing room. "The boss is here!"

Three pairs of sullen eyes turned toward him. "You better have brought us food from your Freezer Day," growled Herb Elliot, his pudgy undersheriff.

"Yeah," agreed his Crime Scene Investigations unit, Byron "Lurch" Proctor, who almost never agreed with Herb Elliot about

anything. Tully had given Lurch his nick-
name. If Lurch wasn't the homeliest person
on the planet, he was at least a contender.
His dull brown hair stood out in all direc-
tions. He wore rimless glasses an inch thick.
His nose appeared to have been attached as
an afterthought, and had been intended for
a much larger person. He was also the
smartest person Tully had ever known. One
whole corner of the briefing room was
Lurch's domain, and he was there most
hours of the day or night. Tully didn't hold
him to a regular schedule, which allowed
Lurch the freedom to work almost around
the clock. The CSI unit appreciated the flex-
ibility. The sheriff, oddly, was the young
man's hero.

"And the food better be something good!"
said Daisy Quinn, her hands planted firmly
on her hips. Daisy was his secretary. Tully
was sure she had been in love with him for
a long time. Well, of course. She was a
woman, wasn't she? Usually, Daisy fairly
vibrated with efficiency, but today she
seemed only to vibrate.

"We're starving!" she cried, a wisp of her
short dark hair bobbing about on top of her
head. She was wearing her tight black skirt
and a white blouse, a combination Tully
thought made her particularly alluring.

Herb Elliot and he had often flirted with Daisy when she was married, but now that she was divorced they both regarded her as somewhat dangerous. It had been months since he had caught Herb perched on the edge of her desk, chatting her up.

"So where's the food?" Herb said.

"It's coming, it's coming. Hold your horses. I've got Buck bringing you each a venison rib. Fortunately, there were four left over."

"He comes through that door with only four venison ribs," Daisy growled, "he's a dead man."

"I figured as much. That's why I got Buck to bring them."

Buck staggered in with a huge, greasy cardboard box. "I could have used a little help, Bo."

"Yeah, yeah, quit complaining, Buck. We've got some starving people here, although you wouldn't know it from looking at Herb."

"Oh!" cried Daisy. "Do I smell garlic shrimp? I do, I do. Oh, all is forgiven!"

Buck spread the feast out on a table. The whole briefing room filled with the smell of garlic.

"Go get the beer, Buck," Tully said.

"Geez, let me catch my breath!"

"Only two bottles apiece. They're still on duty."

"Only two?" Herb said.

"Yeah," Tully said. "It's the Blight Way. Lock the door when you come back, Buck. I don't want any citizens to walk in and catch the staff gnawing ribs and guzzling beer. And tell Flo the feast is about to begin."

"I know already, Bo," Flo said, emerging from the radio room. Her crowning feature was her bright red hair, which seemed almost to have achieved illumination. "By the way, what if there's an emergency?"

"I guess it will just have to wait," Tully said. "We have serious eating and drinking going on here."

Tully walked into his glass-enclosed cubicle. The large window behind his desk looked out over Lake Blight. He was once again thinking about having the window painted over. Because any shooter taking a crack at him in his office chair would have to be bouncing around in a boat a hundred yards out on Lake Blight, only a miracle shot could nail him. But miracle shots were made all the time. On the other hand, he wasn't about to let Lucas Kincaid take away his view. Still, Lucas Kincaid was the kind of nut for whom miracle shots were routine.

Tully would have to think about getting his window painted over. He dialed his phone. A woman answered.

"Agatha, it's Bo."

"Oh, Bo, how nice of you to call. What's the occasion? I know it's still three months 'til quail season."

"The urge just came over me, Agatha."

"She's pretty, isn't she?"

"Prettiest bait I've ever come across."

"Bait? Surely, Bo, you don't think I sent Bunny down to Blight as some kind of incentive to lure you up here to the ranch."

"You pick out the tiny white dress?"

"Well, yes, but . . ."

"I thought so. You're a wicked woman, Agatha."

"Tell me this, Bo. Did it work?"

"You bet. I should be up there sometime tomorrow. Probably bring Pap and Dave with me." He leaned back in his chair, swung his legs around, and planted his boots on the desk.

"Must you bring that nasty man?"

"What have you got against Dave?"

"You know the one I mean. But anything to get you up here, Bo, is fine with Bernice and me."

"How is Bernice by the way?"

"Oh, she's welding up a storm. Wait until

you see what she has done with the front gate. It's gorgeous! And she is so proud of your success as a painter, Bo."

"She taught me everything I know about painting. I suppose she misses all her wonderful students in the U. of I. Art Department."

"Let me say that you are one of the few she mentions, at least without the use of profanity."

"So, Agatha, tell me about this mystery you want me to solve."

"Oh, it's just the foolishness of an old lady, but I've wondered about it all my life."

Agatha said she could not remember her father because she had been only two when he disappeared along with Sean O'Boyle, who was about fourteen at the time. There was little doubt both of them had been murdered, she said, because Tom Link simply wasn't the kind of man to run off and deliberately disappear, at least according to Agatha's mother. All summer, he and O'Boyle had been panning some bits of gold from a creek running down out of the Snowies. Some of the gold still clung to white chunks of quartz, and they thought that it was a good sign it had eroded out of an outcropping somewhere up the creek. They started exploring up along the sides

33

of the drainage and found the outcropping, according to the story Agatha's mother had told her. As they blasted back into the mountain, the vein of gold grew bigger. Tom Link had become increasingly excited about the find and was planning to file a claim. Then, suddenly, he and young O'Boyle disappeared. No trace of them or their mine had ever been found, as far as Agatha knew. Most people thought the mine had simply caved in on them, if there was a mine at all. In those days, it was not unusual for people to disappear in the Snowy Mountains and never be heard from again.

"So, that's the story," Agatha said. "I know it's not much to go on, and I also know I shouldn't be wasting your time on such foolishness."

"Actually, Agatha, I've been thinking about taking a week or so vacation and camping out in the mountains for a while with Pap and Dave. What better time to look around and see if we can find some clues to the disappearance of your dad and the boy."

"That would be wonderful, Bo! You can probably use a little vacation. And maybe it will give you a chance to hide out from that monster, Lucas Kincaid."

Tully rolled his eyes and sighed.

"Bernice is so looking forward to seeing

you, Bo. Bunny too. We mustn't forget Bunny."

No indeed, Tully thought. "Got to go, Agatha, but I'll probably see you tomorrow." He hung up and walked out to the briefing room. "Daisy, as soon as you're done wolfing down that shrimp, get your pad and come in here."

Barbecue sauce still rimmed Daisy's lips when she came through the door. "I suppose it couldn't wait until I was done eating."

"I don't have until midnight," he said. "Now shut the door."

Daisy kicked the door shut behind her and sat down in a chair across the desk from him. "The shrimps are scrumptious! But so are the ribs."

"Good," Tully said. "I'm glad you found something to your liking. Here's the thing. I'm taking a week off starting right now. Pap and Dave Perkins and I are heading up into the mountains for a little camping and fishing."

"Is this about Kincaid?"

"Kincaid has nothing to do with this!" Tully snapped. "I just need some time off, that's all."

He studied the little ring of barbecue sauce around her lips. Kind of cute.

"The deputies are turning over every rock in the county looking for him," Daisy said. "But if you want to hide out in the mountains for a week, Bo, I can certainly understand. He's already killed four people, and that's what we know about. If I were you . . ."

Tully's chin sagged down onto his chest. "One last time, Daisy, I'm not running off to hide from Kincaid. In any case, he's not the kind of person you can hide from. He will find me, no matter what. Maybe that's the plan, if there is a plan. Is that clear?"

She nodded. "But . . ."

He held up his hand to shut her off. "One last time: I'm going to be away fishing and camping for a week. I'm leaving you in charge here. As usual, we'll let Herb think he's running the show, but you actually do it. That's why I pay you the big money."

"Yeah, right. Well, the first thing I'm going to do is make sure all the guys are focused on Kincaid."

"You'll be in charge, Daisy. So you call the shots. But I've got Pugh busy with another project. He won't be available."

She raised her hand like a schoolchild wanting to be called on.

"Yes, Daisy?"

"Will Brian call in, so we can keep track

of him?"

Tully tugged on the corner of his mustache while he thought about this. "I don't know. I'd rather Pugh keep his mind on his assignment."

"It wouldn't hurt for him to call in once in a while, so we know he's all right."

"Why? You got a thing for Pugh?"

"I've got a thing for all our people, in case you haven't noticed."

"Maybe you're getting too soft for this job, Daisy. Anyway, I don't want you to call me unless there's an emergency you can't handle. And you know what of yours gets run through the wringer if things get messed up."

Daisy smiled. "Might be interesting. Can I count on that?"

"We'll see how relaxed I am after this camping trip. I'm going to stop by and see Mom now and then head home to pack up a tent and supplies. After you finish wolfing down your meal, call Pap and tell him I'll pick him up at five sharp in the morning. All he needs to bring are a sleeping bag, the whiskey and cigars, and his portable gold dredge."

Daisy frowned. "Gold dredge?"

"Yeah, it's a little machine you stick its spout down in the riverbed. It sucks up sand

and gravel and sprays it over what amounts to a sluice box. The gold, if any, settles out into the sluice. Makes prospecting a lot faster than panning."

"You want Pap to come armed?"

Tully laughed. "Pap always comes armed, sweetheart. If you had as many enemies as Pap, you'd be armed, too. As a matter of fact, tell him to bring a rifle. Maybe we'll do some plinking at cans or something."

"Plinking, my eye. You're up to something, Bo, and it's got nothing to do with plinking or sleeping on the hard, cold ground."

"Maybe. Anyway, I've got a big favor to ask. I want you to stay nights at Mom's house while I'm gone."

"Oh, my gosh! You think Kincaid might . . . ?"

"I don't know. He's a vicious monster and might think that's a good way to get back at me. I really hate to ask this, Daisy."

"Bo, you know I'd do anything for you."

"Really? Well, maybe we'll discuss that when I get back. Take your service revolver with you. Mom's got a couple of shotguns there and she knows how to use them, but I'd just feel better if you stayed with her."

"Hey, we'll have a ball."

"Probably. But keep in mind Mom can drink you under the table. And don't listen

38

if she starts delving into her raunchy history."

"This sounds better all the time."

Tully drove over to his mother's house. Her car was in the driveway, so he knew she was home. He tried the door. It was locked. He thought this was probably the first time in all the years she had lived in Blight that she had locked her doors. He knocked and called out, "Ma, it's Bo!"

Rose opened the door. "I'm exhausted," she said. "Don't know if I'll ever do your Freezer Day again."

Tully followed her into the kitchen and sprawled on a bench at the breakfast nook. "Who else could I get to run the pie table?"

"Sit up straight, Bo. Ever since Ginger died, your posture has gotten worse by the year. I'm making some tea. You want some?"

"Sure. You got pie to go with it?"

"You're kidding, of course. I made it home with five different kinds: blackberry, chocolate cream, banana cream, lemon meringue, and peach. I'm keeping the peach all to myself. It's made with canned peaches but still yummy."

"Okay, I'll take a slice from each of the others."

"Pick one. You're starting to get a belly on you."

"No way! Besides, I'll wear off any fat the next few days. Pap and Dave Perkins and I are going camping in the Snowies."

Rose cut a piece of the banana cream, placed it on a saucer, and slid it in front of him. "It's the Lucas Kincaid thing, isn't it?"

"No! It's just that I want to get away and relax for a while."

Rose laughed. "You want to get away and relax and you take Pap with you! Ha!"

"I'm taking Dave, too."

"That makes me feel a little better. Dave still pretending to be an Indian?"

"The last I heard. For some reason, he thinks if he keeps up this fraud long enough, I'll start thinking he's a real Indian and he can turn Dave's House of Fry into a casino. But he's a terrific tracker and that's not pretend."

Rose said, "I suspect that for all Dave's joking around, he's about as deadly a human being one is likely to come across. But I've never heard him so much as raise his voice."

"You ever look into his eyes?" Tully asked.

"I try not to. He might get ideas."

"What I came to tell you, Ma, is that Daisy will be spending nights with you until we get Kincaid locked up."

"Oh, Bo, I know you don't have any intention of locking Kincaid up. I wasn't born yesterday, you know. And I was married to Pap quite a few years. But I would enjoy having the company, if Daisy doesn't mind. Besides, I've been thinking of having a little chat with her, now that she's divorced."

"Divorce or no divorce, I don't want you blabbing anything about me to her, you hear?"

"Yes, dear. What are you going to do on this camping trip, anyway?"

"I thought we'd do a little prospecting for gold," Tully said. "You know I've always wanted a little gold mine."

"Gold prospecting! Good heavens! Well, if you find any gold, first thing you do is shoot Pap in the head."

"I don't think my own father would steal my gold."

"Well, shoot him in the head anyway."

"You're a hard woman, Rose!"

After finishing off three slices of pie and two cups of tea, Tully said good-bye to his mother and headed out to his patrol car. It was almost dark. As he started to unlock the door, he dropped his keys and bent over to pick them up. The car window exploded above his head. Seconds later, a car roared off on the side of the block behind his mother's house.

Brian Pugh came running up. "You okay, Bo?"

Tully let out a long quavering breath. "Yeah, but it was close."

Pugh was almost crying. "I know. I'm so sorry, Bo! I was parked down the street and he must have made me. He probably sneaked into the neighbor's backyard behind your mom's house."

"I feel like a sitting duck here in town," Tully said. "Once I get out in the mountains, I'll have a better chance against this maniac."

"It won't take long for him to hear you're camping out in the Snowies."

"Pugh, I think you and I could use a good stiff drink. I'll meet you down at Crabbs Lounge in fifteen minutes."

Pugh stared off into the distance. "I know this can't be good."

"You're right about that."

3

Crabbs Lounge was empty of patrons when Tully arrived. His Freezer Day had wiped out all their usual customers. They were probably all home sucking down Alka-Seltzer. A waiter was sitting at the bar sipping a glass of beer. He made a sweeping gesture. "Help yourself, Sheriff."

"Thanks, pardner. I'll see if I can find an empty table." The man looked vaguely familiar but the light was bad. When you've put away as many criminals as he had, you try to remember faces. Sooner or later the owners of the faces usually get out. He took a table near the back of the room. Pugh came striding in a few minutes later and sat down across from Tully.

"So what's up, boss?"

"You'd better have a drink first." He waved the waiter over. "I'll take a Manhattan. What'll you have, Brian?"

"Make mine a Manhattan, too."

The waiter looked at Tully. "What kind of scotch do you prefer, sir?"

"Any single malt," he said. "But it will be well scotch anyway."

"Right," the waiter said. "I see you've had drinks here before."

He went to get their order.

"So, what brings us here, Bo?"

"It's like this, Brian. I want you to take a little vacation."

"I don't like the sound of this already."

Tully smiled. "Can't I invite one of my favorite deputies out for a drink without him becoming suspicious? I guess not. First of all, let me ask this. Do you have any decent camo hunting clothes?"

Pugh stared at him. "This sounds worse all the time. Yeah, I bought some RealTree last fall."

"Excellent."

The waiter brought their drinks. "In honor of the Bo Tully Freezer Day, the bartender actually used some of his Bushmills."

"Thanks. Tell him I appreciate it."

The waiter smiled and left. Tully searched his memory for a name but couldn't come up with one.

"Go on," Pugh said.

"Here's my idea, Brian. I want you to go hunting."

"I'm way ahead of you on that, Bo. You want me to go into the mountains and hunt down Kincaid."

"You're awfully quick, Brian. I ever tell you that?"

"No, not that I can recall."

Tully smiled. "It's a bit more complicated. Kincaid is out to get me, if the event tonight is any indication. So I have let it be known around town that I'm going to be camped out on Deadman Creek for a week. Kincaid won't have any trouble coming across that bit of information. So I have calculated that will put him in the area of the campsite on Deadman. I need you to be up there waiting for him."

"Why me?"

"Because you're the best hunter and the best shot in the department, that's why."

"And?"

Tully hesitated. "And you don't have a wife or children. Let's face it, Brian, you are expendable."

Pugh sighed. "I have an ex. That should count for something. Ernie Thorpe doesn't even have an ex. Why not him?"

"Ernie doesn't have your experience. Besides that, he's young and good looking and deserves a chance at life. Kincaid would kill him right off, and you know it."

Pugh gave a little laugh. It had a bitter edge to it. "And you think he won't kill me?"

"That's a chance we'll have to take. Hey, Brian, I'm using myself to lure him into range. All you have to do is shoot him."

"I hear he's like a wild animal when he's out there in the mountains."

"That's right, he is. So that's how you hunt him, like he's a rank old buck deer. Take it very slow and easy. Stop and listen every few steps. Don't make a move until you've checked out the next few yards."

Pugh laughed again. "You make it sound interesting, Bo. I notice you left out the part about rank old buck deer generally showing up unarmed."

"Picky, picky," Tully said. "You know that ridge that overlooks the campsite. That would be the best place for Kincaid to take a shot at me. If I were you, I'd watch that ridge. Oh, I forgot to mention that you can put all your expenses on your county credit card. Just don't go hog wild."

"I have to think about it, Bo. I'll let you know in a couple of days."

"That's too late. I need to know now. How about another drink?"

"Sure. But I'll still let you know in a couple of days."

Tully waved the waiter over. "I'm heading

up to Deadman tomorrow. I'll expect you to make the right decision, Pugh."

4

At six sharp in the morning, Tully pulled up and stopped his twenty-year-old 4×4 Ford pickup truck in the paved driveway of Pap's mansion on the hill. He honked the horn, even though the old man was seated on the porch in his Adirondack chair, rocking furiously. Deedee, Pap's young and gorgeous housekeeper, waved at him out the kitchen window, the main reason Tully had honked the horn. He gave her a big smile and waved back. Pap stalked down off the porch carrying a pack, his gold dredge, and other odds and ends. He threw them under the pickup's canopy, then went back and got hip boots and a rifle. He put the boots under the canopy, then got in the cab. He stood the rifle upright between his knees.

"That thing loaded?" Tully asked.

"You bet. A gun ain't much use unloaded. Just one time in your life, Bo, I'd like you to show up when you say you're going to show up. I should know better but I've been wait-ing out on that porch for over an hour, freezing my butt off the whole while. I see you brought along your dog."

Clarence growled at him.

"Growl at me, you little mutt, and I'll pinch your head off."

Clarence stopped growling and lay his head down on his paws.

"I see you're in your usual chipper mood," Tully said.

"You should be glad I'm going along to watch your back," Pap said. "You can bet I'll do a better job of it than Pugh did."

"How did you know about Pugh?"

"He called me up last night and told me what happened. You should of knowed Kin-caid would stake out your mom's house. Just because he's crazy don't mean he's dumb."

Tully backed out of the driveway. "I'm surprised you care. You must be getting soft in your old age."

"I don't care. But it's embarrassing for folks to think my own son ain't any smarter than that. They'll think it's the way I raised you."

"And here you didn't raise me at all. Now fasten that seat belt."

"Folks don't know that." He fussed with

the seat belt. "I hate these miserable things. In a wreck, the only thing they do is make the bodies easier to find."

Tully reached over and snapped the buckle shut. He had never known an old person who could fasten a seat belt. Maybe it was because most of their lives, cars didn't come with seat belts.

"Forget about Kincaid," he said. "We'll stop in Famine and pick up Dave, and the three of us will camp out in the Snowies and do some fishing and gold prospecting."

He glanced at Pap. The old man had taken a little white paper from a package, dumped some tobacco in it, and started rolling himself a cigarette. "No smoking in the vehicle! I've told you that a hundred times!" He backed the truck out of Pap's driveway and headed down the street to the highway.

Pap finished rolling his cigarette and punched in the lighter on the dashboard. "What was you saying? I was so busy rolling myself a cigarette I missed it." The lighter popped out and he lit his cigarette. He blew a plume of smoke at Tully. "You know, it's kind of a miracle, a truck this old and its lighter still works."

"Good point. Maybe it will accidentally become disconnected."

Pap sucked thoughtfully on his cigarette,

then said, "If we pick up Dave, where's he going to sit? On top of the dog?"

"No, I thought we'd stop at Batim Scragg's ranch first and I'd make him a little present of Clarence. Every ranch needs a good dog."

Pap laughed. "You're hard, Bo, truly hard. You put the man's two sons in prison, a reasonable person might think that's enough grief for him, but now you intend to give him this mean little critter to make him suffer some more."

"Being a man of profound ignorance, Pap, you might leap to that conclusion. But I've spent a good deal of time studying both Clarence and Batim, and I've arrived at the opinion they are both basically of the same character. I suspect they'll enjoy each other's company."

"Ha! Clarence bites Batim just once, the old man will shoot him!"

"What's your point?"

An hour later they drove through the little town of Famine. Tully knew that in addition to Batim Scragg's two sons he probably could have put half the town in prison for its part in the same marijuana enterprise. On the other hand, prison would have improved the Faminites' social standing to such a degree he thought it best to let matters remain as they had been for the last hundred years. He couldn't stand the thought of them putting on airs.

Pap studied the various residents they passed. "This is Kincaid's hometown. You figure he's holed up here someplace?"

Tully shook his head. "Naw, he no doubt visits from time to time, but I'm pretty sure he's got a camp up in the mountains someplace. He probably comes in to resupply from time to time, but there's no chance anyone here would squeal on him. Kincaid isn't the kind of person you want to get on the bad side of."

"You mean like throwing him in prison?"

"Something like that."

They pulled into the Scraggs' as Batim was walking across the barnyard with a bucket in each hand. "Howdy, Bo. Pap. You fellas showed up just in time to see my new piggies."

"Piggies?" Tully said, thinking of toes and how gross Batim's must be.

"I love baby pigs!" Pap said. "There ain't nothing cuter than a baby pig. It's about the only animal I have any affection for. Shoot, after I've watched baby pigs for a while I don't eat bacon for a month."

"I don't believe it," Tully said. "Your one weakness is baby pigs?"

"Yep. They're about as cute a critter as you are ever likely to see. Lead the way, Batim."

The pen had about a dozen little pink sausages running every which way, with several of them nursing on their humongous mother, who lay on her side staring forlornly at the side of her pen. I'm with you, Mama, Tully thought.

Pap was delighted. "Look at that little guy playing with a piece of straw! Ain't that the cutest thing you ever saw!"

"This is a whole new side of you I never even suspected," Tully said.

Batim said, "I got to agree with you, Pap. I'm mighty fond of baby pigs myself."

Tully couldn't believe it. Here were two of the deadliest human beings he had ever come across making fools of themselves over a dozen little sausages. He guessed he would never plumb the depths of human nature.

"So what brings you out this way?" Batim asked.

"The main reason we stopped by is I brought you a nice little dog."

"Really? What's wrong with him?"

"Nothing's wrong with him. It's just that I'm away from the house so much I can't take care of him. It really breaks my heart to give him up, but there's nothing else I

53

can do. So I asked myself, who could give Clarence a nice home? That's when I thought of you, Batim." He shot a look at Pap that said if you grin or say one word you're dead. The old man had rolled his eyes toward the sky at first but now appeared perfectly sober. They walked back to the truck. Tully picked up Clarence and set him on the ground in front of Batim. The two of them looked at each other.

"He seems like a nice little dog," Batim said.

Clarence wagged his tail. Batim reached down and picked him up. Tully held his breath. The dog continued to wag. Batim scratched him behind the ears. "Well, sure, I'll take the little guy. I really appreciate you thinking of me, Bo."

"It just occurred to me that you and Clarence had a lot in common."

"So, other than Clarence, what brings you up this way?"

"Oh, Pap and I are picking up Dave Perkins to go camping with us. We're heading up into the Snowies. Going to spend a few days at the campsite on Deadman Creek."

Batim shook his head. "I don't reckon that's a wise move. Kincaid was born and raised in those mountains. He's like a wild animal. You'd be a lot safer in town, Bo."

"Batim, I'm not running off to hide from Lucas Kincaid! If he happens along, I'll deal with him. By the way, you seen anything of Lucas?"

"Sure. He stopped by and visited shortly after he broke out and killed them two guards. If I knowed at the time he had his mind set on killing you, Bo, I'd have put a bullet in him myself."

"I appreciate the thought. Any particular reason he stopped by?"

"He wanted to pick up that stinky old cap of his, the red-and-black plaid one with the earmuffs that tie up on top. He gave it to me down at the jail when he was going to be locked up. I tossed it up on a shelf in the woodshed and forgot about it, figuring Lucas would be gone about forever. Suddenly, he's at my door and wants it back. Says it's his lucky hat. That raised a sweat on me, I can tell you, because for a moment I forgot what I done with it. Then I remembered. That's why I'm still alive, I reckon. That stupid cap apparently means a lot to old Lucas. By the way, I don't think Lucas has ever got next to a bath in his entire life. The smell of him almost buckled my knees. He stops by here again, Bo, you want me to kill him for you?"

Tully pondered the favor for a moment. "I guess not, Batim. That might complicate matters. I appreciate the offer, though. Of course if he were to threaten you, don't hesitate."

"Gotcha. Thanks for Clarence, Bo. I really appreciate it."

"Think nothing of it, Batim. I'll miss him but I know he's going to a good home."

They drove back toward Famine and to Dave Perkins's House of Fry. As usual, the parking lot was full. The House of Fry offered the best and cheapest breakfast within a hundred miles.

"How about you buying me some breakfast while Dave gets his stuff packed?" Pap said.

"If I know Dave he had his stuff packed and ready to go last night. Nothing he likes better than a camping trip."

"He don't seem to like violence. You ever notice that? A fight starts or something, he walks away, gets in his car, and drives off. I seen him do it more than once."

"I don't blame him. You're probably the one in the fight, Pap, or at least the one who started it."

"Not always! I just think it's strange a grown man like Dave walking away from a fight."

"Hard to tell," Tully said. "I think he worked for the government for a while, but he never says anything about what he did before moving to Famine. I suspect it was something that caused him to lose his taste for violence. There are folks like that, you know. Come on, I'll buy you breakfast."

"You're just saying that because Dave never charges us. I think I'll have the chicken-fried steak and hash browns with gravy. The chicken-fried steak is the biggest and best in the world."

"It must be. That's what the sign says. Dave wouldn't lie about a thing like that."

The restaurant was crowded with locals and apparently a few tourists passing through. Tully looked around for an empty table but found nothing. Then a man and his wife at the far end stood up. The man shouted above the roar of chatter. "Here's one you can have, Sheriff! We're just leaving!"

"Thanks, pardner," Tully told him, ambling over.

"I never thought I'd get the urge to eat again after your Freezer Day," the man said, "but danged if I wasn't hungry again this morning."

"Glad you could make it," Tully said. He and Pap pulled out chairs and sat down. A

57

pretty waitress came over, cleaned off the table, and returned with a couple of menus. She gave Pap a big smile. "You want the seniors'?"

"No, miss, I still go with the regular. The white hair is just part of my costume. What's your name anyway?"

"Everyone calls me Missy."

"Well, Missy, you are the prettiest girl I've seen in a long while."

"Why, thank you!" she said, just as if she hadn't heard the same thing from a hundred customers. She disappeared into the kitchen.

Dave Perkins walked over and sat down. "I wondered when you two characters might show up. I've got my stuff ready to go."

"You packin'?" Tully asked.

"Armed to the teeth."

"Good."

The waitress came back to take their orders. Pap went with the chicken-fried and hash browns with gravy. Tully had two hotcakes and bacon.

"How can you eat bacon after seeing them little piggies?" Pap asked.

"Piggies?" Dave said.

"Yeah, Bo drove out to Batim's place and gave him Clarence and we got to see his piggies. I tell you, Dave, they are about the cutest little critters you ever seen."

"Piggies?" Dave said.

When the waitress returned, she gave Pap another big smile.

"Missy," Dave said, "I don't want you flirting with this old reprobate. He came by last fall and ran off with my prettiest waitress. Said he needed a housekeeper! He's nothing but a vile old man and you best avoid him."

Missy laughed and returned to the kitchen. Pap watched her go. "I tell you this, Dave," he said. "Deedee turned out to be not such a bargain as a housekeeper. She bosses me around from morning to night. You can have her back anytime."

"Really?" Tully said. "And here I thought you were in love with Deedee."

"What's that got to do with anything? I'm in love with lots of women, but I can't stand being bossed around."

"It's their nature," Dave said. "I'd think you'd know that by now, Pap. So, what's this I hear about us stopping by Quail Creek Ranch?"

"I thought we should stop for a visit," Tully said. "I haven't seen Agatha and Bernice since the last time we went quail hunting up there. You know they're both getting well up in their eighties."

"Right," Dave said. "Now tell me about the girl."

"What girl?"

"There's got to be a girl."

"Oh, well, I do recall something about Agatha's niece staying at the ranch while Agatha helps her with her dissertation for a Ph.D."

"I thought so. Pap, this girl is a knockout, right?"

"Knock you right out of your boots, Dave."

"Hey," Tully said, "this trip is not about women. It's to get off by ourselves in the mountains, do a little fishing and gold prospecting, and just generally relax."

"So why is it we need to be armed to the teeth?" Dave said.

"I'll let you figure that out for yourself."

"Yeah, everybody around here knows Kincaid has sworn to kill you, Bo. Half the town is rooting for him and the other half for you. So your idea is to lure him out into the mountains."

"That's right. And arrest him."

"I bet. You figure if he shoots you, Pap or I will get him."

"That's not why I'm taking the two of you."

"You mean, what if he shoots Pap and me

first? He knows we're both better shots than you."

"Now you're starting to get the idea."

5

Tully turned off the highway, and the truck bounced and twisted the three miles up the rutted dirt road to Quail Creek Ranch. An iron gate blocked the ranch's driveway into the house.

"Hey!" Dave said. "Look at that!"

Half a dozen metal quail rose in flight across the bars of the gate.

"Pretty spectacular," Tully said. "But I expected it to be. Agatha already told me about it. She said Bernice had started working on metal sculptures this past year and the gate was her first project. You know they were both my professors at the U. of I., don't you, Dave? Bernice in art and Agatha in English."

"Both of them are pretty famous as I recall," Dave said.

"They really are. Agatha once even gave a lecture at Oxford. I guess the deans there are about the worst audience in the world.

If they don't like something they yell the speaker down and beat on their desks with their walking sticks or whatever they can find. And they don't like much of anything. But they gave Agatha a standing ovation, something no one had ever heard of before at Oxford."

"Pretty impressive," Dave said.

"Oxford," Tully said. "That's in England, Dave."

"I was wondering about that."

"Me, too," Pap said.

Tully and Dave burst out laughing.

Dave got out and opened the gate, and Tully drove through. The hills on both sides of the narrow valley were dry and barren except for sagebrush, rabbit bush, coarse grasses, and outcroppings of reddish rock. The narrow valley itself was lush and green. Quail Creek, almost hidden by alder and birch, assorted bushes, and thick patches of ferns, trickled over rocky beds and around small gravelly beaches. The branches of the large birch trees met overhead and created a green, leafy tunnel through which shafts of light penetrated and danced on the water.

Dave got back in. "The next gate is yours, Pap."

Pap said, "Since you have to get out to let me out, you might as well open the gate yourself, Dave. By the way, this is the most beautiful ranch I know. I offered to buy it once, and the ladies said they would sell it to me but they got to live on it until they died and after that I could have it. I said, 'No way,' figuring they wouldn't kick off until after I did and I'd be out the money."

"Good figuring," Dave said. "The last I saw them, both Agatha and Bernice were still going strong. Looked like they might live forever."

Tully said, "Bernice is a full-blooded Cherokee, you know that, Dave?"

"Yeah, we talked about it one time. She was interested in my Indian heritage."

Tully laughed. "Your heritage is fake Indian. You tell her you discovered you were part Indian when you came up with the idea of turning that restaurant of yours into a casino, how you're the only member of the Dave tribe?"

"I may have neglected some of the details. Until you prove differently, though, I'm sticking to my heritage."

Agatha and Bernice's house was low and sprawling and appeared almost to be growing out of the ground. Bernice came out of the broad doorway of the hay barn wearing a long leather apron and a red-and-blue bandana wrapped around her head. Her hair was long, totally white, and tied back in a ponytail. She waved and smiled and came toward them, taking off large leather gloves as she walked. "Bo, it's so good to see you." She threw her arms around him and gave him a hug so vigorous he could feel his feet almost leave the ground. She shook Dave's hand and gave him a big smile. "I'm so glad you could make it, Dave." She stood back and studied Pap, then yelled toward the house. "Nail down the furniture, Agatha, Pap Tully is here!"

"Very funny," Pap said. "The only thing I've ever seen around here worth stealing is that gate of yours. I'll probably sneak up here some night and relieve you of it. It's much too nice a gate to leave in the possession of two vile old women."

Bernice laughed. "I think there was a compliment hidden in there someplace." She gave him a playful hit on the arm. "You must be getting soft in your old age, Pap."

"That gate is truly a wonder," Dave said. "It's certainly worthy of the best quail hunting in the state."

"Why the three of you get so much enjoyment out of killing those poor little birds I'll never know, but I guess it keeps the quail and chukar populations under control. If any of you were better shots, I might start

65

to worry."

Agatha came out of the house and stopped. She put her hands on her hips and gave them a big grin. "I had no idea my bait would work so fast!"

Tully walked over and gave her a hug. "Bait?" he said. "What bait? By the way, is Bunny around?"

Both Bernice and Agatha burst out laughing. "Not at the moment," Agatha said. "She drove into Angst to get some more printer paper. She's closing in on that dissertation of hers. It's wonderful, by the way, a study of the works of Rachel Carson and particularly the effects of *Silent Spring* on the use of pesticides. We probably wouldn't have any birds left now, except for that book. We still have eagles dying of lead poisoning, of course!"

"Always the bird-hugger!" Pap said. "I see you ain't changed one bit, Agatha. You put your poor niece up to this mischief, knowing Bo's weakness for beautiful women."

"Pap, I can't believe you would accuse me of such a reprehensible ruse. Anyway, you look as robust as always. Quite remarkable, considering that gorgeous housekeeper of yours. I really expected you to be dead by now." She put quotes in the air around the word "housekeeper."

"Actually, Agatha, I was going to mention Deedee. Now that you're old and on the verge of senility, I would be most happy to lend her to you. Permanent! I'd even continue to pay her wages."

Agatha pondered the offer for a moment. "I'll have to think about that. Hey, it's wonderful to see you fellows, even Pap. Come on in. I'll have lunch on the table in a minute or two."

Lunch consisted of an exceptionally tender roast, potatoes, carrots, onions, and gravy.

"Looks delicious," Dave said.

"Thanks. It's my Crock-Pot special."

Tully forked a piece of roast into his mouth and chewed it contemplatively. "I thought it was a bit dark for beef," he said. "This is venison."

"Right you are, Bo," Agatha said. "We had our garden out back all fenced in, posts and wire six feet high, but even so, every morning when we got up a deer would be in there munching it. We raised the top of the fence by two feet and plugged every gap, but no matter what we did that deer somehow managed to get in. I swear, if we planted the garden on top of the barn, that deer would show up with a ladder. Finally, Bernice had her fill of him. She grabbed her rifle and plugged him right in the middle of the garden."

Tully glanced at Bernice. She appeared slightly uncomfortable. "According to my calculations," he said, "gardens and deer season don't occur at the same time."

"It was a very late growing season," Bernice said. "Please pass the butter."

A car pulled into the yard's driveway and sent a spray of gravel flying. Tully's hand slid under his vest and he half rose to peek out the window. Then he relaxed and sat back in his chair. A minute later Bunny Hunter came through the door carrying a bag of groceries and a couple of other packages. She was wearing jeans, a blue work shirt, and leather boots. Some blond hair drifted across her face and she blew it back with a puff from the side of her mouth. "Aha!" she said. "I see I'm late for the festivities."

All three men rose from their chairs as if on command, possibly in recognition of her startling beauty.

"Oh, please be seated!" she said. "Are you trying to embarrass me? Bernice and Agatha treat me like a ranch hand. I'm not accustomed to manners."

"I set a place for you, dear, right next to Bo," Agatha said.

"Has he displayed any of his charms?"

"None that I've noticed."

"Well, okay then." She sat down. "Good to see you guys."

Tully introduced her to Dave.

"I've heard a lot about you, Dave," she said. "Well, actually, mostly about your chicken-fried steaks. The House of Fry happens to be Agatha's and Bernice's favorite restaurant."

"They obviously are ladies of impeccable taste."

"Have you always been in the restaurant business?"

Tully and Pap were suddenly interested.

"No, this is my first restaurant. Before that I kind of kicked around the world, which was interesting, but then I got the urge to settle down. Famine struck me as the perfect little town."

"Kicking around the world sounds wonderful!" Bunny said. "I wouldn't be wild about living in Famine of all places, or any one place in particular. I would love to travel, though, but I can't afford it."

"It never used to be so expensive," Dave said. "I lived on a beach down in Mexico for a while. It was wonderful and cost practically nothing. I made myself a little hut to sleep in and fished off the beach at night. The locals called the fish *pargo,* but they looked like red snapper. I coated them with coarse salt and roasted them on a stick over charcoal, just as I had seen a woman in a beachfront café do it. They were delicious! The café had a thatched roof and no walls, only posts, and sometimes the ocean would wash across the floor and I and the other patrons would lift our feet and go on eating, and then the water would recede and we would put our feet back down. I doubt a person could do that anymore, live down there in a hut on a beach. But just talking about it makes me want to go back."

"I lived in Mexico for a while," Pap said. "The people were great."

Tully thought he should mention that was when the FBI was after Pap on numerous corruption charges, but he decided to restrain himself. Furthermore, nothing was ever proved on the corruption charges. He said, "Agatha, it's time you filled us in on the mystery."

"Oh, dear!" she said. "I know it's a bunch of foolishness, but I've wondered about my dad's disappearance my whole life. Did he just run off and leave us, or did something happen to him and his helper?"

Bunny and Bernice got up and cleared the table, while Agatha went on to tell them as much as she knew about her father, all of which came from her mother, some old friends and neighbors, and a few faded photos. She got a photo album off a shelf and opened it on the table. One picture showed her father, Tom Link, with a teen-age boy. Both were dressed in jeans and work shirts. Neat handwriting in pencil on the back identified the boy as Sean O'Boyle, age 14. Another photo showed Sean posed with a pick over his shoulder. "What's that white thing behind him?" Tully said.

Agatha said, "It's so out of focus I've never been able to make it out. It's odd, though, because those rocks on the edge are sharp. It could be a patch of snow on a steep hillside."

"Can I take that picture with us?" Tully said.

"I had a copy made for you," she said. She handed Tully the copy wrapped in plastic and then went on with her report, as methodically as if she were giving a lecture. Having read over her mother's diaries numerous times, she had by now all but memorized them.

Tom and Sean had camped out in the Snowies all one spring, panning for gold in various streams. One day they found a stream with bits of gold in it. Some of the gold had white quartz still clinging to it. They followed the gold upstream and found a small outcropping of white quartz. Upon close inspection, they found thin veins of gold threaded through the outcropping. They began blasting away the outcropping and following the gold. They worked all that summer on the mine, and the veins of gold grew thicker the deeper they blasted into the mountain.

"As a matter of fact," Agatha said, "I have a piece of quartz my dad brought home shortly before he and Sean disappeared." She went into her den and returned carrying a white rock the size of a baseball. She handed it to Tully.

"Holy cow!" he said. "Look at this." He handed the rock to Pap. Dave stood up and looked over Pap's shoulder. "They was getting into a major strike," Pap said. "If anyone ever found that mine, people would have heard about it."

Agatha explained that Tom and Sean blasted a very small opening to the mine, just high enough to get their wheelbarrow through to dump the tailings from inside. Whenever they left, they covered the opening with brush and pieces of driftwood. Once they were a few feet inside the mountain, they blasted a tunnel large enough to stand up in. When they hit the main veins of gold, Tom started talking about filing a claim. A few days later they disappeared.

Agatha said, "There's one big gold mine over in that area of the Snowies, but it's been shut down since the 1940s. Now with the price of gold going through the roof, you would think someone might try to open it up again, but I guess the shaft and tunnels are all rotted and caving in. I hear it would be just too dangerous and expensive to open them to mining again. But no one has ever found a single sign of my dad's little mine. It's just as if it vanished from the face of the earth."

"How did Tom and Sean supply their mine?" Tully asked. "They had to haul in blasting powder or dynamite, food, tools, camp gear. They didn't haul all that in on their backs."

"No," Agatha said, "they hauled it in with a team of horses and a wagon. Then Sean drove the team back to the ranch, because there was no place to keep the horses near the mine. Then he walked back to the mine."

"Sean do all this in one day?"

Agatha thought for a moment. "Mama kept a lot of it in her diary, but I never paid much attention to the details." She went into her bedroom and returned with the diary. "Here's what she wrote about a month before Papa and Sean disappeared." She read a passage that said Tom and Sean had taken a wagonload of supplies to their mine that morning, starting right after Tom had milked the cow. The boy had returned with the wagon late that afternoon, eaten dinner with Agatha's mother and the baby Agatha that evening. He spent the night at their house. In the morning, he milked the cow, ate breakfast, and walked back to the mine.

Tully stared at the ceiling. After a bit, he said, "Anybody know how fast horses walk?"

Bernice said, "I can Google it for you."

"That would be great. While you're running your computer, Bernice, I'll go get a topographical map I have in the truck."

By the time he returned with the map, Bernice had finished Googling.

"How far to the base of the Snowies from here, Agatha?"

"Exactly fifteen miles. We've checked it on the car speedometer. The road runs straight from the ranch over to the Snowies. It intersects there with Hastings Road, which runs along the base of the mountains."

"I know Hastings Road," Tully said. "I've fished those creeks many times. Did Google know how fast horses walk?"

"It said five, which I assume means five

miles an hour."

"Great!" Tully spread the map out on the table. He drew a square on it. Dave stood up and peered over his shoulder.

"Okay, here's the ranch," Tully said. "It's fifteen miles over to the base of the mountains. That would take three hours, with the horses pulling the wagon at five miles an hour. After they reached the base of the Snowies, they could have turned either north or south at Hastings Road."

Tully frowned. He tugged on the corner of his mustache to help him concentrate. "Okay, let's assume they turned north on Hastings. They get to the drainage where the mine is located and unload the wagon. They can't leave the team alone on the road and they can't leave supplies stacked in view for somebody to come along and steal them. They have to haul them back into the woods and out of sight. Tom then packs the supplies up to the mine while Sean drives the horses and wagon back to the ranch."

Pap got up from the table and walked over to look out a window. "I can't stand this," he muttered.

Dave said, "Let's say it takes three hours to drive to the mountains at five miles an hour and an hour to unload the wagon. That's four hours. It takes Sean three hours to drive back from Hastings to the ranch. That's seven hours. Sean is gone a total of about ten hours. So he spent a total of three hours going and coming on Hastings. Divide that in half. It took them an hour and a half to drive up to the drainage where the mine is. At five miles an hour, that's seven and a half miles from the intersection with Hastings."

"That's about what I calculate," Tully said.

"Me, too," Pap said. "Of course, they could have turned south."

Tully put his finger on the map. "Don't complicate things, Pap! This will at least put us in the ballpark of where to look for the mine. The mine was either within a range of seven and a half miles north of the intersection with Hastings or seven and a half miles south."

He ran his finger along the road on the map. "There are two small drainages and one big one in that seven and a half miles north of the intersection. Deadman Creek flows out of the big one right at the end of that section." He tapped his finger on a symbol. "Look, there's a mine symbol on top of the ridge above the second drainage. I'll bet it's a gold mine, too."

Agatha looked at the map. "Yes, it's the Finch Mine. It's owned by Teddy and Margaret Finch. I know both of them well. The family shut the mine down over fifty years ago, but all the buildings are still up there. It was quite an operation."

"Yeah, it was," Pap said. He walked back to the table and looked at the map. "When I was just a mite, my daddy worked there for a couple of years. He'd bring me home pieces of rock and I'd pound it up with a hammer and get bits of gold out of it. I put the gold in an empty ketchup bottle. I must have had a couple ounces of gold in that bottle, but when we moved away I forgot all about it. Every once in a while I think about going back up to the mine and seeing if I can find that bottle. But they've got a heavy chain and a lock on the road and No Trespassing signs all over the place."

Dave laughed. "You let No Trespassing signs keep you out, Pap? I find that hard to believe, given a person of your character."

"Actually, I usually forget to bring my bolt cutter when I'm up this way. Fortunately, I had the good sense to bring it along this time."

"About what I figured," Tully said.

"I suppose I could have parked my truck at the chain and walked in but the road is pretty steep from there on," Pap said. "Now that we've got the area narrowed down to seven and a half miles, we should turn up Tom's mine in no time. How long are we going to spend looking for this mine, which may not even exist?"

"Who knows?" Tully said. "I'd be glad to leave you here with Agatha and Bernice. They could find some chores for you, right, Agatha?"

She put her hands on her hips and looked at Pap. "Oh my, yes, we certainly could use an old reprobate to pull some knotweed for us. We've been getting a terrible infestation of it the last few years."

Pap straightened up and stretched. "Too bad, Agatha, but this old reprobate has got to go help these boys find a lost gold mine."

Tully folded up his map and looked at Agatha. Somehow in the past few moments she seemed to have shrunk. Maybe it was a change of light in the room. Her wrinkles seemed to dominate her face, even framed as it was with a halo of white hair. "What's wrong, Agatha? You look worried."

"Bo, I just thought about that madman that's after you. And I noticed you reached under your vest when Bunny's car drove into the yard. You have to be awfully concerned about that monster. So, here I am, asking you to go off on a frivolous goose chase just for me. Kincaid could be out there in the mountains waiting for you."

"Agatha! Agatha! Agatha! The last thing I ever want to do is cause you the slightest worry about me. As far as Kincaid goes, we're getting that problem taken care of. I've got Pap and Dave with me, and you know they're a whole lot more dangerous than Kincaid. If the three of us can't handle that nut, I'd better look for another kind of work. I may not have mentioned this to Pap and Dave but I've got one of my best deputies concentrating on Kincaid and we've worked out a little trap for him."

Pap looked surprised. "We have a plan? Don't tell me it involves Pugh! Our lives depend on Pugh?"

Bernice put her hand on Tully's cheek. "Bo, I wish you would give up this job. You know you could make a nice living now as an artist and you wouldn't have some maniac out to kill you."

"Probably only art critics then," Tully said. "But right now I'm up here to enjoy myself, and there's nothing I like more than delving into a mystery, particularly one provided by you, Agatha."

"You're sure, Bo?" she said. "You're sure you wouldn't rather be out there trying to arrest Kincaid?"

"Arrest Kincaid? I'm absolutely sure of

that, Agatha. Anyway, there's one thing I've been wondering about. How did you and your mother survive here on the ranch after your father disappeared?"

"It wasn't easy," Agatha said. She told them how her mother had been teaching all eight grades at the Boulder Creek School when she married Tom Link. The school was one room and built of logs. It was three miles from the ranch. After Tom disappeared, her mother went back to teaching at the school. She would get up at four, milk the cow, fix breakfast, bundle Agatha up, and drop her off at the O'Boyles', who lived between the ranch and Boulder Creek. Then she would walk on to the school, build a fire in the stove, dip a bucket of drinking water out of the creek, and get ready to teach the dozen or so kids in eight different grades. At noon, she would cook them hot lunch from government commodities and then read to them from Mark Twain or Jack London or one of her other favorite authors, and finally start the afternoon session. She would pick up Agatha from the O'Boyles' that night and walk home carrying the little girl, milk the cow, and cook supper. "That's the way it was in those days," Agatha said. "People did what they had to do."

"Just like nowadays," Tully said.

Pap snorted. "I hope you're joking, Bo. It ain't the way it is nowadays at all! Now gov'ment rushes in and gives out handfuls of cash! It's terrible!"

"Oh, for the good old days," Tully said.

6

They arrived at Hastings Road by early afternoon. "What's the plan?" Dave said.

"The first thing we better do is set up camp on Deadman," Tully said. "I've camped there lots of times over the years. There's a great campsite at the end of an old logging road. The high country above it is about as rugged as I've ever seen. I got lost up there on a hunting trip twenty years ago. Thought I was going to die, but I worked down to the headwaters of the creek and managed to find my way out."

"Didn't happen to see a gold mine, did you?" Dave asked.

"Afraid not. Most of my attention was used up staying alive."

"Deadman," Pap said. "The name has a nice ring, don't it?"

"It's the biggest stream," Tully said. "Probably run your dredge and find some gold there, Pap. The logging road is drivable at least as far as the campsite."

Dave nudged Bo in the ribs. "Better take a look in your rearview mirror."

"I've been watching it." He pulled over to the edge of the road and stopped.

Pap grabbed his rifle. "What you watching?"

"There's a vehicle following us," Dave said. "Hangs there about half a mile back. Now that we're stopped, it stopped. It's about the size of a BB."

"The size of a BB!" Pap said. "That's small enough we could tromp it to death." He opened the door and stepped out.

"It's a blue Ford pickup," Tully said. "I make it out to be an '85 four-by-four with a dented left fender."

"Man, either you have eyes like an eagle," Dave said, "or you're totally full of it."

"Check it out, Dave. There's a pair of glasses in the glove compartment, if you're hard of seeing."

Dave grabbed the binoculars, stepped out of the cab, and stood next to Pap. He brought the binoculars to his eyes and brought them into focus. "He's just sitting there, watching us."

"What kind of vehicle?"

"Looks like a blue pickup," Dave said. "Ford."

"How about the dent in the left fender?" Tully asked.

"I can't see that even with the glasses."

"And you call yourself an Indian!"

"Forget what I call myself," Dave said. "I was thinking Kincaid might be tailing us. Maybe he followed us all the way to the ranch. A guy like Kincaid could kill Agatha, Bernice, and Bunny just to pass the time until he could get a shot at us."

"You're right, Dave! That's exactly what Kincaid would do." Tully dug his cell phone out of the glove compartment and dialed. Daisy answered.

"Bo! It's about time you called!"

"Why? What's up?" He could not still a cold shiver that ran through him.

"Just about everything. An old couple in a cabin up on Woods Lake have been murdered. Family members found them this morning, both of them shot to death. Whoever did it took several guns, the couple's car, and some other stuff, according to people who knew them."

"What kind of car?"

"A red Humvee."

"Put out an APB on the car. Tell the state patrol I'd like a couple of troopers patrolling the highway to Angst and ten miles beyond and to be on the lookout for that red Humvee. He may have switched cars by now, though."

"You think Kincaid killed them?"

"Kill an old couple for their car? Sounds just like him. He would do it for sport. Now here's what I want you to do. I know you're spending nights at my mom's house, but I want you to drop everything and get over to her place right now. Take your gun and don't bother coming into the office tomorrow. Stay at Mom's until I get back. You understand, Daisy?"

"But what about the office?"

"Flo can run it from the radio room. Herb can do whatever Herb does, but he's to stay in the office night and day. Now get me Lurch."

"Lurch is up at Woods Lake doing the cabin."

"Okay. Where's Thorpe?"

"Ernie just came in."

"Great! Tell him to get up to Agatha's ranch pronto. Run flat-out and emergency all the way. I want him armed to the teeth. You can tell him how to get there and to stay until he hears from me."

"Will do. I don't know where Pugh is. He stopped by the murder scene at Woods Lake earlier and nobody has seen him since. I hear he was shaking with rage when he left."

"Don't worry about Brian. I've got him busy. At least I hope I have."

"Be careful, Bo!"

He could tell she was upset. "Don't worry, sweetheart. We'll get this under control pretty fast."

He punched off and dialed again. Bernice answered.

"Bernice! Listen, I never meant to get you and Agatha and Bunny involved in this, but that maniac who's trying to kill me, if he thinks you're friends of mine he might try to kill you ladies just for the heck of it. If he followed us he may know where you live. Both Agatha and you know how to handle guns and maybe Bunny does, too. So get yourselves armed. He may be driving a red Humvee. And he's probably wearing one of those stupid caps with the earmuffs tied up on top."

"Those caps are great, Bo! Don't call them stupid, because I wear one myself when I'm hunting."

"Sorry about that, Bernice. I'm sure you look lovely in your hat. But if a guy shows up at your door wearing one, kill him."

"What if it's the wrong man?"

"I'll take care of that later."

"Is that what you call the Blight Way?"

"You got it, Bernice. The Blight Way.

Another thing. I've got one of my deputies, Ernie Thorpe, headed up to the ranch to stay with you. He's a young, good-looking guy and should be wearing a uniform. Don't shoot him. He'll stay with you until we take care of this maniac that's running around. See you soon, Bernice." He punched the off button.

Pap stuck his head in the cab. "The pickup is just sitting there, Bo."

"Yeah, I see it. We better get up Deadman a ways and make camp. You still have enough daylight to check the creek for gold."

Tully almost missed the turnoff to Deadman, the road was so grown up with brush and small trees and some trees not so small. He plowed into the road anyway, then stopped. "Pap, get out and turn the hubs. We have to four-wheel it from here."

"How come I got to do all the work? Next time, Dave can set next to the door!" He climbed out and turned the hubs, then climbed back in and started to roll himself a cigarette, possibly as an act of revenge.

First Kincaid and now I got Pap trying to kill me, Tully thought. The truck growled ahead through a narrow green tunnel of brush and trees, branches scraping both sides and screeching like a large animal in serious torment.

Dave said, "After this I'll be surprised if you have any paint left on your truck."

"It's the latest style, especially in twenty-year-old Idaho pickups. I'll sell it to you cheap when we get out of here, Dave."

"If we get out of here!"

"If we don't, I'll sell it to you even cheaper."

7

After twenty minutes of plowing through brush, Tully turned the pickup down toward the creek. They suddenly emerged into a park-like area beneath giant hemlocks. Pap, grumbling, helped Tully pitch his white-wall hunting tent with the stovepipe of his sheepherder stove running up through the roof. Tully set up three cots inside, laid foam pads on top of them, and spread sleeping bags out on the pads. Dave cleaned out the old fire pit, lined it with new rocks, gathered up several armloads of dry wood, and dumped them by the pit. Pap sat on a log and bossed. With the camp set up to his satisfaction, he put on his hip boots and plodded down to the creek to try his gold dredge.

Tully tied back the canvas door flaps to air out the tent. They were already hot from the sun. Tully loved the smell of hot canvas. Then he walked over to inspect Dave's fire pit and woodpile.

Dave said, "I'm wondering if it's such a good idea for us to be sitting around a campfire at night. Kincaid could sneak in here and blast us."

"Anything's possible," Tully said. "You get out away from the hemlocks, though, and the terrain is steep and thick with brush and generally pretty nasty, even for Kincaid." He pointed through a narrow opening in the trees to a bare ridge overlooking the camp. "My guess is he would slip in up there. The shot would be three hundred yards but a piece of cake for Kincaid. He would have a clear shot and probably could even fix himself up a rest for the rifle. But you have to remember it's me he's after. With the three of us sitting around the campfire at night, he wouldn't be able to tell me from you or Pap. Say he shoots you first by mistake, Dave. Pap and I would dive for cover and grab our rifles."

"Why me?"

"Why do you think I brought you along?"

"I did wonder."

Tully laughed. "I'm not letting Kincaid or anybody else prevent us from enjoying our campfire. If he's even following us, it would be well into the night before he reached the ridge. It's a rough climb to get up there, but it's the only place he would have a clear shot at us."

Dave looked up at the ridge. "That's a pretty long shot. You sure Kincaid could make it?"

"He could make it, all right. That's why I was thinking of letting you wear my vest."

"Your bullet-proof vest? Mighty thought-ful of you, Bo."

"No, my regular sheriff's vest, the one with the big star on it. You would look good in it, Dave."

"That's about what I expected."

Pap came tramping into camp. He laid his gold dredge down on the ground, flopped into a camp chair, and began rolling down his hip waders. "Nary a speck of gold. I sucked sand and gravel out of the cracks of a big old flat rock that practically spans the whole creek. If any gold washed down Deadman's in the last thousand years, I would have picked up a bit of color at least. Nothing."

"Maybe some other prospector sucked it out before you," Dave said.

"Naw, they never get it all. I'd have got a speck or two, at least."

"We're not up here to get gold anyway," Dave said.

"That's not the idea," Tully said. "Tom

and the boy would have panned the creek to see if they could find any gold. If they found some, they would work their way up the drainage until the color ran out. Then they would have started looking around on the side hills to see where it was coming from, the mother lode so to speak. Obviously, they found it. That's where Agatha's chunk of quartz came from. If Pap can't suck up any sign of gold in Deadman that means we're in the wrong drainage."

"So I guess we'll move camp tomorrow."

"Naw, we'll keep it right here. This is the perfect spot."

"You're getting weirder every day, Bo. So who brought the single malt this time?"

As Tully explained, Pap was in charge of bringing the whiskey and cigars because he was rich. He also brought the steaks and potatoes, wrapping the latter in foil, sliced and buttered and alternated with onions for roasting in the fire. They sat around the fire and sipped Bushmills and smoked cigars after finishing supper.

"I think these cigars are Cuban, Pap," Dave said. "Don't you know they're illegal?"

"I never heard that. You heard that, Bo?"

"Can't say I have, Pap, but I'll check on it as soon as I get back to the office. If they turn out to be contraband, I'll have to put you in prison and confiscate all your cigars."

Before they went to sleep that night, they heard an owl hoot. Pap said he'd once heard an owl call his name.

"That's bad news," Tully said. "That means you're going to die."

"I was three years old and I ain't dead yet. What do you think of that?"

"Maybe it meant the owl would die."

"Well, if this one hoots all night, he's going to die."

Tully was awakened later in the night by what he first thought was a large animal attacking a small woodland creature. Loud snarls followed by pitiful squealing filled the tent. Then he realized it was Pap and Dave snoring. He pulled his sleeping bag over his head and went back to sleep.

Tully got up early the next morning and caught a dozen small rainbow trout for breakfast. He grated three large potatoes into his cast-iron frying pan, chopped up a large onion, mixed it in with the potatoes, and made hash browns. Then he spread a dozen strips of bacon into another frying pan and cooked it crisp. He forked the bacon out onto a paper plate, rolled the trout in flour, salted and peppered them, laid them in the hot bacon grease, and cooked them until they were golden brown.

Pap came yawning out of the tent. "I thought I smelled bacon frying. Yup, by golly, I did. Fish! You know how to lift an old man's spirits, Bo, I have to admit that. You must have got up at the crack of dawn."

"Yeah, I did. As a matter of fact I was awake long before dawn cracked. Your and Dave's snoring kept me awake most of the night. I think you were the little woodland creature and Dave was the huge beast tearing the little guy to pieces."

"You must have been dreaming," Dave said, coming through the tent flaps. "I've never snored in my entire life. If you want to call those pitiful squeaks and squeals that come out of Pap snoring, well I guess you've never been in the army and lived in a barracks."

"I'm afraid I came up between the wars. It wasn't easy. You've got to have good judgment about when to get born these days. So how many trout, Dave?"

"Three and a small mountain of those hash browns. They look yummy."

"Yummy! I've never heard a grown man say 'yummy.' "

"You have to be awfully tough and mean to say 'yummy,' Bo. I've been places where saying 'yummy' could get you killed."

"You're close to being in one of them right now." Bo slid three small trout and a mound of hash browns onto Dave's plate. The trout were brown and crisp.

"You eat them like French fries, Dave."

"I already figured that out. They're about the size of fries."

Pap had been paying serious attention to his own plate of bacon, trout, and hash browns. He looked up. "I just had an idea."

Tully and Dave looked at him as if this might have been Pap's first idea in years.

"So?" Tully said.

"You know that mine that was marked on the map? That's the Finch Mine. It's only a couple of miles from here. Why don't we go take a look at it?"

"Let's see," Tully said. "Well, it's within the range we figured out. But you said there's a chain across the road and No Trespassing signs all over the place."

"I told you I snuck a bolt cutter into the back of the pickup. We can just snip the lock off and drive on in. It won't hurt nothing and I can look around and see if I can find where I buried the bottle of gold."

"You sure that's the same mine Gramps worked?"

"Yeah. It won't hurt nothing for us to go in and take a look. We're just messing around anyway. You know there ain't no way we're ever going to find out what happened to Agatha's pappy and that boy. It's over eighty years since they disappeared."

Tully tugged on the droopy corner of his mustache while he mulled this over. "I'll tell you what, Pap. I'll call Agatha and see if she can tell me where the Finches live. If she can, we'll go ask them if we can look around the mine."

"There's one big drawback to that approach. They might say no."

Tully took out his phone and dialed Agatha.

"Bo?" she said.

"Yeah, it's me."

"I thought you'd be calling. Your deputy showed up last night. I almost shot him, but he's much too good looking."

"Despite Ernie's looks, he's a pretty good deputy. He'll stay there until we get Kincaid run down. He won't be much of a bother."

"Oh no, he's a lovely young man. He and Bunny have hit it off, too."

"What! Put Ernie on. I need to have a word with him."

"He and Bunny are out by the creek. I'll have him call you when they come in."

"Yeah, please do, Agatha. Oh, the reason I

called — can you tell me where the Finches live?"

"Why, yes, Teddy and Margaret Finch are good friends of ours. They're a lovely couple. You would never know they're filthy rich. They own thousands of acres of prime timber land and they keep their woods like a park. A year or two ago, Teddy got some ecological award for his stewardship of the land or some such thing. They know all about you, too, Bo. They're some of your biggest fans."

"My sheriffing? I didn't know law enforcement had fans."

"Of course not, silly. I mean your painting!"

"Oh, good. Maybe they'll let us go in and check out their mine. By the way, tell Ernie I don't hold with poaching."

"Poaching? What on earth do you mean?"

"Ernie will know. So tell me how to get to the Finches' place."

"It's about three miles on the other side of Angst, a huge white house with a white board fence out front that encloses about twenty acres. You can't miss it."

"That their pasture?"

"No, dear. It's their front yard."

"Thanks, Agatha. Talk to you later." He closed his phone.

Pap was finishing off the hash browns. "She tell you how to get to the Finches?"

"Yep. Saddle up and let's go."

8

The Finch place had about half a mile of paved driveway. On one side was the Finch lawn and on the other was a pasture with a dozen or more beautiful horses prancing about. Tully hated horses, but if he ever started to like them he thought he would probably like one of these.

Pap said, "If Finch sold those horses he could buy the whole town of Blight City."

"If he sold one of them," Dave said, "he could buy the whole town of Blight City."

"I wonder where Teddy made his money," Tully said.

"He didn't make it at all," Pap said, squishing out a hand-rolled in the ashtray. "His daddy didn't make it, either. It was his granddaddy, Jack Finch, made all of it on that gold mine we're going up to see. He took millions and millions and millions in gold out of that mine. When the ore played out, his son and grandson invested the money in timber. Got their own sawmill around here someplace. One of the few mills in the country that still turns out prime lumber."

"How come you know so much about it?" Tully asked.

"I'll tell you how come. Back when your granddad was sheriff, old Jack Finch apparently got the notion that some of his business associates was trying to kill him. He talked to my daddy about it and paid him a sizable fee and your grandpap took care of the problem. I don't know how exactly, but your grandpap wasn't nothing like you, Bo."

"That's what I understand. As a matter of fact, you're nothing like me either, Pap."

"I didn't want to say it, knowing how tender your feelings are."

Tully got out of the pickup and walked up to the front entrance. A tall, slim, white-haired man answered the chimes. "Yes, sir, what can I do for you?"

"I'm Sheriff Bo Tully of Blight County and —"

"Good heavens!" The man called over his shoulder. "Margaret, we have a celebrity right here at our own front door — Bo Tully!"

"I don't believe it!" the woman cried. "Bo Tully, the artist?"

100

"I don't imagine there's more than one Bo Tully. Come in, sir, come in! Oh, I see you have a couple of folks in the truck. Tell them to come in, too."

Tully signaled Pap and Dave to join him. The man stuck out his hand. Tully shook it. The grip was surprisingly strong.

"I'm Teddy Finch. This is my wife, Margaret." Mrs. Finch was tall and willowy, with her silver hair wrapped up in a bun and held with a pin.

Mrs. Finch said, "We are so delighted, Mr. Tully. We have been fans of your painting for many years. You can't believe what an honor it is to finally meet you!"

Tully introduced Pap and Dave, who now seemed somewhat subdued to be in the company of such a famous person.

Mrs. Finch said, "Come in, come in, please, gentlemen. Teddy will show you into the sitting room and I'll go fix a pot of tea." She disappeared into the vast spaces of the house. Tully had expected a butler to appear at any moment, along with a maid in a short black dress and a white frilly apron. Apparently, Finch read the expression on his face. "You're wondering why two old people are living in this gigantic house alone. It wasn't so large when we had our five children here and my father and mother, both of whom passed on quite a few years ago. Back then we did have some service people, mostly for my dad to torment — at least that was my opinion at the time — but now it's just Margaret and me. We prefer it that way, as long as we can do for ourselves."

Dave took Pap's hat off his head and handed it to him. The three of them sat down on a couch across from Finch. "What brings you all the way up here, Sheriff Tully? I hope we haven't broken any laws."

"Not at all, sir. Actually, the three of us are up here on vacation," Tully said. "My father here is an amateur gold prospector and is fascinated by old gold mines. He was wondering if you would give us permission to look around the old Finch Mine."

"I don't see why not, as long as you promise not to sue me if you fall down an empty shaft. Seriously, the whole underground system is rotten. There may still be some gold down there, but it would be too expensive to get to. I'm not a miner anyway."

"Oh, we just want to look around," Tully said. "My dad lived in one of the houses up there when his dad worked in the mine back in the thirties."

They went on discussing the mine until Mrs. Finch came in with the tea and some crumb cake. "You all had the good fortune to arrive on one of the few days I happened to do some baking," she said. "When we're done with the tea, I want to show you some of the Bo Tully watercolors we have bought over the years. We just love your paintings, Mr. Tully. When are you ever going to give up law enforcement and become a full-time painter?"

"Maybe the next election," he said. "You never know about voters."

Finch laughed. "I don't think you have to worry too much about elections anymore, not with the popularity of the Bo Tully Freezer Day."

"Oh, that has nothing to do with politics," Tully said.

"Right," Finch said, still smiling. "You fellas believe that for a second?" he said to Pap and Dave.

"Not for a second," Dave said. "Bo may seem lackadaisical, but he never makes a move without planning it out in detail first. Never ask him to explain anything. He will bore you to death with the details."

Pap said, "You mind if I have another piece of that crumb cake, Mrs. Finch?"

"Goodness no," she said. "I'm just delighted you like it so much."

"As soon as your father finishes with his cake, I'll show you all around," Finch said.

"Besides Bo Tully paintings we collect a few other things."

"Oh, show Dave and Bo around, Teddy. Pap and I will just chat. I want to know what he's been up to since he's no longer sheriff himself."

"You remember when I was sheriff?" Pap said.

"I do indeed! Those were such wonderful times, all the gambling and drinking and dancing all night. I remember when you killed those three bank robbers and got shot yourself. You were such a hero! I just loved it all!"

Pap beamed.

Finch took Dave and Bo into a large adjoining room and pointed up to shelves along the walls near the ceiling. The shelves were lined with dozens of baskets and clay pots. "These are mostly from coastal Indians, but the ones in the next room are from interior tribes, the Spokanes and Coeur d'Alenes and some Kootenai and Nez Perce."

"They're wonderful," Dave said.

"They're mostly Margaret's doing, but they keep her occupied. Now, step into my den and I'll show you what interests me." He led them into the den, the walls of which were covered with firearms, including a blunderbuss.

Tully pointed at the blunderbuss. "Don't tell me that's an original."

Teddy reached up and took the gun down. He handed it to Tully. "Oh yes, they're all originals. I'm afraid I can't take the credit for collecting them. That was the work of my grandfather Jack Finch, but I love looking at them and thinking about where they've been and how they were used. No doubt they killed a great many people."

Tully handed the gun back and Teddy replaced it on the wall. "I've never before held that much history in my hands. I could almost feel it flowing through me."

Teddy nodded. "I get the same feeling myself."

"What kind of man was your grandfather?" Tully asked.

"I remember him as a tall, handsome man, with a sweeping mustache not unlike your own, Bo. He was always nice to me in his old age, but I guess he was pretty fierce when it came to some others. My father, Theodore, would go pale and start to tremble at the mere mention of his name, and that was after Jack Finch had been dead for a good many years. Jack rode with Teddy Roosevelt's Rough Riders. Roosevelt was his hero. Thus the name Theodore for my dad and me."

Tully looked around at the guns on the wall. "Well, I've got to tell you, Mr. Finch, I've never seen so many old guns in one room in my entire life!"

"Oh," said Margaret, coming up behind them, "you should see the basement. It's crammed full of guns."

Tully gave her a surprised look. "A basement full of guns?"

"Yes," Finch said, "but most of them are not nearly so impressive. There might be a few gems down there, but I've never worked up the enthusiasm or the energy to sort them out. Almost all the guns came from my grandfather, the ones here and the ones in the basement."

"All from your grandfather?" Dave asked. "He must have been quite the sportsman."

"I never knew him well," Finch said. "But I doubt Jack was much of a sportsman. As I say, my father was scared to death of him."

"Jack sounds like my kind of man," Pap said. "My own daddy was sheriff and my grandpap before him. Both of them knew your dad and your granddad, too. They was real men back then."

Finch nodded. "I think you may be right about that, Mr. Tully."

Partly to keep Pap from revealing anything

more about the family, Tully said, "We shouldn't take up any more of your time, Mr. Finch. If you will just give us the key to the mine chain, we'll be on our way."

"Oh dear," Finch said. "It has been so long since any of us has been up there, I'm not sure where the key is right at the moment."

"We got a bolt cutter in the truck," Pap said. "What say we just snip the padlock off and put another lock on when we leave. We can drop the new key off here when we head home."

"Bolt cutter?" said Finch. "Why, that's a good idea."

On their way to the Finch Mine, Tully stopped in Angst and did some shopping, including the purchase of a new padlock. He would just as soon Pap had kept his mouth shut about the bolt cutter, but it had probably saved them some time. He returned to the truck and put his purchases under the canopy. Pap and Dave were outside, Pap smoking, Dave leaning against the truck, his hands in his pockets. "You fellows want to grab some lunch, or will that crumb cake and tea hold you 'til supper?"

"I vote for lunch," Pap said. "That was the worst crumb cake I ever ate."

"I agree," Dave said. "So why did you take a second piece?"

"I was trying to be polite," Pap said. "Besides, Margaret and I had a nice little chat. She said old Teddy is quite the greener. He still has his men log steep slopes but leave enough trees for the canopy to shade the slope and slow the snowmelt. They don't have a single stream in their woods that's been silted in or flooded out."

"There's a rarity," Tully said. "This whole county used to be prime fly-fishing, but most of it is gone now. Take a thousand years for it to come back."

"What good will that do?" Dave said. "We'll all be dead by then."

"That's why it will come back."

9

A sign on the door of Jake's Café advertised that lunch was served between eleven and two. "This look okay to you guys?" Tully said.

"No, but it will do," Dave said.

"Must be the hot place to dine in Angst," Tully said. The café was empty. All the tables were covered with red-checked oil-cloths, most of which had bare spots that had apparently been peeled by bored diners. They sat down at a table in the middle of the room. A chubby waitress in a dirty apron came over and gave them menus. "What's good?" Dave asked.

"Nothing, actually," she said. "But most everything is edible. The Canadian stew ain't bad. I recommend it along with the vegetable medley."

"What roughly is the Canadian stew?" Tully asked. "I can guess at the vegetable medley."

"Sliced potatoes, onions, carrots, cabbage, and other stuff plus slices of something that passes for beef and all of it covered with gravy so you don't have to look directly at the ingredients."

All three took the Canadian stew, vegetable medley, and beer. The beer was cold and good and served in the bottles without any glasses to fuss with. Pap said it dampened down the remnant taste of the crumb cake. The waitress brought them a plate of rolls and a dish containing a slab of butter.

They were sprawled back in their chairs drinking their beer and waiting for their Canadian stew when the two loggers came in, or at least two husky young guys who looked like loggers.

"We got somebody sitting at our table, Stubb," one said.

"They'll just have to move, Gordy."

"Afraid not," said Tully. "There are plenty of empty tables left. Make one of them your special table."

Stubb said, "Either you move or we'll move you."

The waitress came over and said, "Stop causing trouble, you clowns. Go sit at another table. These guys ain't bothering you."

Stubb said, "Mind your own business, Bev."

"Okay, I'm moving this one," Gordy said. He bent down, grabbed Dave around the waist, and started to lift. Tully became interested. Dave gave him a questioning look.

"I'll give you a hand," Stubb said, bending over to grab Dave around the neck. A second later both loggers were out cold on their backs, bleeding about the face. Dave hadn't risen from his chair. Tully wasn't even sure he had seen him move.

"I hate it when somebody ruffles my shirt," Dave said. "I have to iron them myself and it's a big nuisance."

"Remind me not to help you out of your chair," Tully said.

"You didn't learn that move in no army," Pap said. "I was in Korea and we never learnt nothing like that."

"Different time, different army," Dave said.

Bev brought out the Canadian stew and vegetable medley and another round of beer. She stepped over Stubb, set the tray on the table, and distributed the plates and silverware. The cook came out of the kitchen. "I'm Jake," he said, wiping his hands on what may have once been a white

111

apron. "Lunch and beer are on the house." He nodded at Stubb and Gordy. "I never seen nothing like that before, a guy who could put Stubb and Gordy out cold without even getting up from his chair."

"Thanks, pardner," Tully said. "We appreciate the offer, but we'll pay. This stew is delicious."

"Don't think too bad of them," Jake said. "Logging around here has totally tanked. Stubb and Gordy haven't worked in months. It makes some guys stupid or crazy, I don't know which. They're not bad boys."

Stubb and Gordy, occasionally emitting groans, remained on the floor until lunch was finished. As Tully got up to leave, both loggers began to shows signs of life, much to his relief. Pap left fifty dollars on the table to pay for the stew and tipped Bev a hundred dollars. "This is for the nuisance," he said, indicating the two bodies. From her expression, Tully guessed Bev had never before been tipped a hundred dollars. He thought she was about to cry. For a good three or four minutes, Tully felt somewhat fondly toward Pap.

Before heading up to the Finch Mine, Tully pulled into a parking lot and went in to a small grocery to pick up a few staples to tide them over the next few days. He put his selections in a shopping basket and set the basket on the counter in front of the cashier. She seemed tired and worn down by life, but her face brightened when she looked at him. "You're Sheriff Bo Tully, aren't you?"

"Yes, ma'am, I am he."

"Oh, what I would have given to have you in here this morning! I tell you, I never felt so close to pure evil! It was standing right where you are right now. Cold as ice, he was, and I figured he was about to ask for all the money in the cash register. Well, he didn't. He just counted out a bunch of rumpled dollar bills and coins 'til they covered his bill. I couldn't say a word, I was so scared. After he left, I had to go set down, to settle my nerves, and it wasn't 'til then I noticed the smell, I had been so unnerved. It was ghastly, Sheriff! I don't think that man, if that's what it was, ever had took a bath in its entire life!"

Tully tugged on the droopy corner of his mustache. "I think I know the individual you've described. Was he by any chance wearing a cap with earmuffs tied up on top?"

"Come to think of it, he was! That had plumb slipped my mind but you're exactly right, he was! Is he some criminal you're after, Sheriff?"

He looked at her tag. "Yes, he is, Shirley. You would make a good detective. I guess you don't get the *Blight Bugle* this far north."

"Oh, we get it here at the store but I don't read it. Mostly newspapers just upset me."

"You've got a point there, Shirley. I may give them up myself. By the way, can you tell me what the man bought?"

"Now that you mention it, yes. It was kind of weird. He bought a big bag of dried beans, another one of rice, and about ten pounds of salt."

He thanked her for the information, picked up his sacks, and walked out to the truck.

"Guess what, boys," he said to Pap and Dave. "Kincaid was in the neighborhood. From what he bought, though, I think he may be heading back in the mountains to stay. He bought ten pounds of salt for one thing, which makes me think he's planning on making jerky, probably smoking it over a willow fire. I wouldn't be surprised if he has two or three wickiups hidden away back in the Snowies."

"Wickiups?" Dave said. "What are those?"

Tully explained they were a bunch of poles stacked together in the shape of a teepee. "They're not as classy as a teepee, but you

114

can still build a fire inside. Anyway, my plan may be working. Otherwise, he wouldn't be in this area. I don't know if that's good or bad, but you fellas better be on your toes from now on."

"Why did that bit of news just send a chill down my spine?" Dave said.

"What worries me is nobody has heard from Brian in days," Tully said. "I've expected him to call, but nothing."

Pap said, "You think Kincaid might have killed him?"

"I don't want to think about it," Tully said.

10

They stopped in front of the chain at the Finch Mine. Beyond it, up a hill and a dusty road, they could see a large structure open on three sides. It contained massive vats that were staggered down the slope, apparently so the top vat could feed into the next one down, and it into the third.

"What's that little building with the big pile of stuff alongside it?" Dave asked Pap. "The mine's privy?"

"Naw, it's the assay shack."

"That's a relief. What's the big pile of stuff?"

"Slag."

"Look at those vats!" Tully said. "They must have processed the gold right here."

"Yeah, they did some," Pap said. "I think they concentrated it before it was hauled to the smelter. They had sulfuric acid or something in the top vat to separate the gold from the rock."

"I didn't expect such a big operation," Tully said. "I really hate this."

"You hate it?" Dave said. "How come?"

"Because it diminishes my whole idea of gold. It's the only legal currency you can find in nature. You reach down and pick up a tiny piece of it and you can walk into a store and use it to buy a loaf of bread. A forty-niner in California could wash up a pan of the stuff and go buy himself a farm. To tell you one of my secret desires, Dave, I've always wanted my own little gold mine, nothing atrocious like this — something where I could whack a chunk of ore out of a mountain, crush it up and pan out the gold, take in a few hundred dollars a day without too much work. It's a one-to-one ratio for making a living. Otherwise you've got to go to school and then to college and then go to work for some giant corporation with folks hounding you night and day, something like we're looking at right here."

Dave nodded and smiled. "Or you could take up painting and sell your pictures for thousands of dollars. That's pretty much a one-to-one ratio for making a living."

"It's okay but not nearly as good as picking gold up off the ground. Ever since I first heard about them I've envied those forty-niners."

"You could rob banks," Pap said. "That's pretty much a one-to-one ratio for making a living."

"The field's too crowded," Tully said. "It's hard to find an opening. Anyway, I'm amazed and disgusted at the size of this operation."

"Oh, yeah, it was big," Pap said. "When we lived here they must have had at least a hundred men working the mine and the processor. It was a pretty exciting place, with lots of fights and the occasional shooting. Those boys were a tough lot. I loved living up here. I'll get out and snip the lock. I've had a lot of experience with bolt cutters."

"Needless to say," Dave said.

They drove in past the shack with the large gray pile.

Dave said, "Old Jack Finch must have taken tons of gold out of here to have an operation like this."

"It don't look much different from when I was a little kid," Pap said. "Been closed down over fifty years and it's hardly aged a bit."

"Where's the entrance to the mine?" Tully said.

Pap had him drive around to another large structure on the far side of the site. They followed a set of wooden ties Pap said had once supported the rails of a narrow-gauge railroad track. "The tracks were for the ore cars. They hauled the ore from the mine to the processor."

They came to a timber-framed tower. Pap said it was a Galena shaft hoist for hauling the loaded ore cars back to the surface. A large two-sided building stood next to the hoist. It was filled with huge engines, winches, and wire cables, all thick with rust. Tully parked the truck, and they walked up to the edge of the shaft, which appeared to have been dynamited shut. Far down below they could hear the sound of running water. Pap said the winch would lower the workers on a kind of elevator and bring up loaded ore cars. The tracks took the cars to a crusher, where an auger of some sort carried the crushed rock up to the top tub.

"Good thing they blasted the shaft shut," Pap said. "After all these years I imagine the whole thing is loaded with rot."

"I never heard of rot in mines," Dave said.

"Well, that's what I've heard happens in these old mines. You want to test it, Dave, wiggle your way down through those broken timbers and give a loud yell."

"Naw, I'll take your word for it, Pap. So where are the cabins you lived in when your

119

dad worked the mine?"

"I thought I'd see them by now. It's been over sixty years since I've been up here. Maybe they've all been torn down. Let's go look up behind the processor building."

"You go look, Pap," Tully said. "See if you can find your gold bottle. Dave and I will wander around for a while."

Pap went off grumbling that he didn't know why he had to do all the work and if he did find his gold he wasn't sharing any of it as he had intended.

"Yeah, right," Tully said. "Here I've been holding my breath waiting for Pap to share his gold."

Dave chuckled. "Probably not a good idea. Holding your breath, I mean."

Tully and Dave walked back to the vat structure and explored it. It appeared to have deteriorated little. "Why do you suppose they shut down the mine?" Dave said.

"Don't know. Probably ran out of good ore. Back in the fifties I think they were getting only about thirty-five dollars a troy ounce for it."

"Troy ounce?"

"Yeah, there are only twelve troy ounces in a pound instead of sixteen."

"How come? Seems kind of unfair to miners."

"Beats me," Tully said. "You think I'm some kind of mining engineer? What I can't figure out is how anyone knows where to put a mine. Do they just start digging and hope they hit something? Maybe nowadays they have something that sniffs out gold from an airplane, but I'm sure they didn't have anything back when they dug this mine. According to Pap, the shaft went down hundreds of feet before it tapped into the ore."

"Let's climb up and look in the vats," Dave suggested. "Maybe they forgot and left some gold in one of them."

"Good idea!"

They were still examining the vats when they heard Pap shout. He climbed up to them, wheezing but grinning. "I found it!" he gasped. He held up a ketchup bottle half full of dirt. The bottom third of the jar glinted with gold.

"The way I remember, I had the bottle practically full of gold, but I guess if anyone had found it, they would have taken all the gold instead of just two-thirds of it."

Dave bent down to examine the bottle. "Looks like a bunch of little gold beads."

"That's what it is. It's from the assay shack."

Pap explained that the assayers would

weigh out a certain amount of ore and put it into a furnace. When the furnace melted the ore, the gold went to the bottom of the container, but it bubbled and popped and flung little beads up into the melted rock, the slag. When the slag cooled, the assayers would whack it with a hammer to separate the slag from the gold. Then they tossed the slag out the window of the assay shack and weighed the gold to see how much they were getting for some amount of ore.

"My daddy would bring me home a piece of slag in his lunch bucket, and I would sit out in the yard and pound it up into a powder and pick out the gold beads and put them in my ketchup bottle."

"So how much you figure your bottle is worth?" Dave asked.

"Feels pretty heavy."

"Dibs!" Tully yelled.

"Not on your life."

Tully looked out over the sea of mountains spreading away to the north. There was not another structure of any kind to be seen. "Tell me this, Pap. How in the world did old man Finch know to put his mine in this particular spot?"

Pap thought for a moment. "I reckon he started out panning for gold in that crick down in the drainage and turned up some color. So he knew the gold was coming from somewhere. He probably found an outcropping of some kind with bits of gold in it. Then he figured if he blasted his way down from the top of the mountain, he might tap into the mother lode. That's my guess. Gold mining was always kind of a guess, a big gamble."

"Must be a creek of some kind down in the drainage on either side of the mountain," Dave said. "Any chance there would still be signs of gold down there?"

"If there was ever any gold in one of those cricks, we'd still find some," Pap said. "A lot of folks have portable gold dredges these days and work the cricks pretty hard, mostly as hobbies but always hoping to make a big strike. There ain't much chance of getting rich anymore, but my heart jumps every time I turn up a speck of gold. Once you got gold fever, there ain't no cure for it."

Tully walked over to the edge of the ridge and looked into the drainage to the north. Far down below he could hear water. He walked back to where Dave and Pap were waiting for him by the truck. "Doesn't sound like much of a creek down there, but there's water of some kind. It might be kind of tough working our way down from here, but what else do we have to do tomorrow?"

"We could hide from Kincaid?" Pap said.

"This will be as good as hiding from him. Kincaid isn't so stupid he'd think we would go down and explore this creek."

"I seemed to miss something in that comment," Dave said. "By the way, what are we looking for, Bo?"

"A gold mine. Why else do you think we're up here, except to solve Agatha's mystery."

"Oh, I forgot."

"You guys are loony," Pap said. "You'll make good prospectors."

11

Having spent the evening sitting around the campfire smoking cigars and drinking Bushmills out of tin cups, Pap and Dave slept in the next morning. Tully emerged from the tent, shading his eyes from the rising sun with one hand. A rifle cracked above him. He dived past the fire pit, hit the ground rolling, and curled up behind one of the hemlocks. He had a dull pain in his right side and thought he had been hit by a bullet. Then he realized he had landed on part of the pile of firewood. Pap and Dave sprinted from the tent in their underwear, each crouched low and carrying a rifle. The shot was still echoing back and forth up the canyon. It had come from the direction of the ridge.

"Are you hit?" Pap yelled.

"I don't think so," Tully gasped, holding his hand on his ribs. No blood. A good sign. He squinted at Pap and Dave. They had both flattened themselves into the soft moss of the ground behind him. "I don't think he's all that picky right now," he choked out, rubbing his side. "He missed me, so he probably would just as soon take one of you."

"You sure he missed?" Dave asked. "You look like you're in pain."

"Yeah, I dived on top of your woodpile, Dave. I doubt he missed by much, though."

"Where was he?" Pap asked.

"Had to be up on the ridge. That's the only clear shot. Maybe this wasn't such a good idea. I thought I had it figured out."

"You had an actual plan?" Dave said.

"Yeah. I thought it was a good one, too."

"So what are we going to do now, move back to town?"

"I'm a sitting duck in town. You guys can head in if you like, but I'm staying here."

"Sound good to me," Pap said. "That camp cot is killing my back."

"No way," Dave said. "Both of us are sticking with you. But we can't stay here. My idea is we move up to the mine. He would have a lot harder time getting a shot at you there."

"Sounds good to me. Kincaid's already missed me twice. I don't think he will miss a third time. Hand me one of those rifles and I'll cover the ridge while you two pack the truck. Don't worry about the tent. Leave it. We can stay in one of the cabins at the mine. Moving up there is a good idea. It'll give us a little time to think anyway."

Driving out of the Deadman drainage, Tully said, "Either of you have any thoughts about what might have happened to Tom and Sean?"

"From what Agatha told us," Dave said, "I think they must have been killed together. Could have been an accident. Maybe some of their dynamite blew up. Wouldn't be the first time dynamite got touched off by mistake. If it was a whole box of dynamite, there wouldn't be any pieces left to find."

Tully said, "I tend to think it was an accident myself. Still, if we could at least find the place it happened, we should be able to find tools or something, some kind of evidence. I know we're just fooling around while thinking we may get a crack at Kincaid, but we might as well do something."

"I don't think I can stand too much more of this," Pap said. "Why don't we just make up a story about finding the place where they were killed? Maybe say we found a bone or something and let it go at that."

"A bone?" Tully said. "What kind of bone?

127

Any bones left out in the open for eighty years or so would be long gone by now."

"How do I know what kind of bone? You're the genius detective, Bo, the fellow who almost got his self shot because of his stupid idea."

"It was at least an idea. And Kincaid fell for it. It's just that my timing was off."

They had turned back onto Hastings Road and driven a quarter mile when Dave yelled, "Stop!"

Tully hit the brakes. "What now?"

Dave racked a shell into his rifle and clicked off the safety. "Back up!"

Tully backed up. "What?"

"Look over there in the woods."

In the shadows behind of a patch of trees, Tully picked out the shape of a vehicle — a red Humvee.

"I may have forgotten to mention this," he said, "but somebody killed an old couple up at Woods Lake and stole their red Humvee."

"Kincaid," Dave said. "That's the sort of thing he would do."

"The Humvee means he's still up on the mountain," Pap said. "We could wait here and nail him when he comes back for it."

Tully said, "He won't come back. He'll stay in the mountains now. That's where he's most comfortable."

"You think he's got any idea we're headed for the Finch Mine?"

"I doubt it. He may think we'll go back to our camp, because the tent is still there. Maybe he'll hide out up by the ridge, hoping to get a clear shot when we go back for the tent."

"We're going back for the tent?" Pap said. "As far as I'm concerned, that tent is history."

"Why is he so intent on killing you, Bo?" Dave said. "Does he think you'll catch him and send him back to prison?"

"Hard to tell what a person like Kincaid thinks," Tully said. "Or if he thinks at all. That's one of the things that makes him dangerous. You can't guess what a man is thinking if he doesn't think. What concerns me most now is what has happened to Pugh. I should have heard from him."

12

Dave got out of the truck and padlocked the chain after they had driven through. Even though Kincaid could step over it if he wanted to, the chain for some reason made Tully feel more secure. They drove up past the large structure containing the vats; Pap pointed out an overgrown road that led up the hill to the cabins, and Tully drove up it. Considering that the cabins hadn't been used for over half a century, Tully thought they were in remarkably good shape.

"I've slept in worse motels," Dave said.

"Just hope it don't rain," Pap said. He pointed to a cabin halfway up the row. "That's the one we lived in. I found my gold bottle about ten feet out from the back porch."

"You claw it out of the ground with your fingers?" Tully asked.

"I was prepared to, but walking in, I found a shovel with the handle rotted off. Let's don't stay in our old cabin, though."

"How come?" Tully said.

"I don't know why, but it would give me the creeps, staying in there now."

"I didn't know you were superstitious, Pap," Dave said.

"I ain't, but I shoved open the door and went in a ways and I'm not fooling, I got this sudden chill. I thought my hair was going to stand on end. Maybe something happened in that cabin after we moved out. Shoot, maybe something happened in it while we still lived there. I ain't sleeping in our old cabin tonight, I can tell you that!"

"Me, neither," Tully said.

"Ditto me," said Dave.

They hauled their sleeping bags, cots, and foam mattresses into the very last cabin in the row. Tully built a campfire in what had been the front yard, and they roasted smoked elk sausages on willow sticks and ate them wrapped in pancakes Tully had fried in the cast-iron skillet. Dave said he thought it was one of the best meals he had ever eaten, but that was after he had drunk half a tin cup of Bushmills.

The next morning Tully awoke first and thought about jumping on top of the old man to scare him. At the last moment he remembered that Pap often slept with a loaded .357 Magnum pistol on his chest when camping out. They ate canned fruit cocktail out of their tin cups for breakfast. Pap said he usually shot anybody who tried to make him eat fruit cocktail whether or not it was out of a tin cup, but for some reason it tasted pretty good that morning.

"You boys hear the owl last night?" Pap asked.

"No, it say Dave's name by any chance?"

"Better not have," Dave said. "If I thought I was going to go, I'd make sure I took an owl with me. If you think it was the same owl as the one at Deadman camp, that would be spooky. He would have to be following us. In that case, I think I might do him just on principle."

"Naw, leave him alone," Pap said. "He was just doing the usual owl talk. You don't have to worry, Dave, except I don't know what Bo has thought up for us."

Tully told them his plan even though he was making it up as he went along. They would hike down into the drainage a mile or so up the ridge from the mine. Pap would leave the dredge behind but take his gold pan along to see if he could turn up any color. This was at least on the edge of the range the O'Boyle boy could walk in eight to ten hours. It was likely Tom and the boy prospected this creek before Jack Finch showed up. Maybe they could at least find some signs of a camp or old diggings of some kind. He hated to admit it, but he always enjoyed a search, if only for his mislaid car keys.

"I take it you're not too worried about Kincaid showing up around here," Dave said.

"No, if he's still after me, he'll be up on the ridge at Deadman, waiting for us to pick up the tent. For the first time in my life, I have to agree with Pap. That tent is history."

"Sounds like littering to me," Dave said.

"You some kind of greener, Dave?"

"Only when I don't have some maniac out in the mountains trying to kill me. You can leave that tent anywhere you please, as far as I'm concerned."

"Kill you, Dave! I never even thought about him killing you."

"I figured you hadn't."

13

They hiked up the ridge to where Tully thought the creek would get its start, probably from springs. When Dave and Pap complained, he told them this extra effort would give them easier access to the creek, once they got through the dense second growth of jack pine. The trees were so close together Tully thought he might have to turn sideways to get between them. Pap wore his old stained Stetson hat, Dave, a long-billed cap, Tully, his floppy brimmed explorer's hat. They were all dressed in jeans and work shirts and wore White's work boots, which they'd had built for them by the White's Boot shop in Spokane. Tully wore a belly pack. Pap carried only his gold pan. They went down the steep hillside single file with Tully first, Dave next, and Pap last.

The pines' ragged branches scratched and tore at them but thinned out halfway down the slope, which had grown steeper every ten yards or so. Then they came to the blowdown. Apparently, years before, a tornado had hit the slope, ripped up massive trees, and thrown them down in a gigantic version of pick-up sticks. To make matters worse, new trees had grown up through the blowdown. Tully had been through worse terrain, he thought, but he couldn't remember where. When at last his downward progress appeared totally blocked, he climbed up on a large log and walked it until it crossed another log, and then he walked that log, jumped to another log and still another log, most of them wide as sidewalks, most pitched sharply down the slope. He looked back to see if Dave and Pap had followed his lead. Dave was jumping from one log to another, but all he could see of Pap was his head protruding above a high log and one leg and one arm thrown over it. His mouth was working furiously. Tully was glad he was too far away to hear because he already knew more obscenities than he could ever use. Dave turned around and went back for Pap, pulling him up over the log and taking the gold pan from him. Then he yelled at Tully to wait for them. Tully sat down on a log, his feet dangling eight feet above the ground.

The two stragglers finally caught up, Pap still spewing profanities. A branch had caught his shirt and torn it nearly in two. The torn part draped down his back. "Bo, this is absolutely the last time you get to lead me anywhere!"

"Hey, this is my first time here, too," Tully said. "What am I supposed to be, some kind of psychic? Anyway, this is the end of the blowdown and it can't be much farther to the creek. The slope is starting to level out. Looks as if we have to fight our way through some tall brush. Once we get to the creek, though, I figure the water will be shallow enough we can wade down it and stay out of the brush."

They dropped down from the last log of the blowdown and began pushing through the brush, which clawed at them from every angle. Pap had apparently run out of his vast stock of profanities and now was reduced to groans and yelps. Then they came to the devil's clubs, thick as hair on a dog's back, as Pap claimed. Tully himself had never seen devil's clubs so thick and with such large, sharp thorns, and for the first time he fully appreciated the name. Then, suddenly, they were at the creek. He sighed with relief as he pulled himself loose from the last of the devil's clubs and stepped into the shallow water. Pap and Dave came thrashing their way in after him.

"Yoweee!" Dave cried. "I never knew they made water this cold."

"Don't worry about the cold," Tully said. "Pretty quick you'll be outfitted with poor man's insulation."

"What's that?"

"Numbness. Your feet will be so numb in a minute you won't notice the cold."

"This water must have been ice ten minutes ago," Pap growled.

"Cold is very soothing to the feet," Tully said. "So stop complaining. At least it's shallow, scarcely over our ankles."

"Yeah," Dave said, "but it's also pretty wide. What happens if it gets narrow?"

"What happens if another stream feeds into it?" Pap said.

"I've never known such a couple of worry-warts! You already should have your poor-man's waders and now you're worrying about something else. What more do you expect to happen?"

That's when the mosquitoes found them. The hum of the black cloud of villainous insects was almost deafening. They were so thick around Tully's face he was afraid of inhaling them. Clearly, the tiny beasts hadn't found another source of nourishment all spring and now three major banquets miraculously appeared. Pap tried to pull his torn shirt up to cover the exposed portion of his back but his face and hands were already black with mosquitoes. He killed them by the dozens with each swat of his hands.

"So much for outdoor adventure," Tully said. "Well, there's no point in just standing here, waiting to be eaten alive." He struck off down the creek followed by Pap and Dave. They had moved scarcely fifty yards when a stream from a spring fed into the creek. The spring bubbled up out of a clay bank, and the three of them smeared their faces and arms with thick layers of clay. Tully even smeared Pap's exposed back. The clay worked, and the mosquitoes soon gave up and moved away in search of easier victims.

"See," Tully said. "Just leave it to the old woodsman to fend off irritations of the wilds."

"Irritations!" Pap said. "I'm already a quart low on blood! I would have thought the old woodsman might have remembered mosquito netting or mosquito dope."

Dave said, "How come the tallest, best-looking guy with the best hair always gets to lead? I'd rather follow someone who knows something."

"If you're just going to complain about piffling details, Dave, shut up. I'm trying to identify that sound."

The three of them stopped splashing through the water and listened. "Sounds kind of like a waterfall," Dave said.

"You'll notice steep rock cliffs have closed in on each side of us," Pap said. "I don't like the sounds and looks of any of this."

Tully scratched a piece of moss and a small stick out of the clay on his face. The sun was now beating down into the canyon and drying the clay. He glanced at Pap and Dave, much as he hated to. The clay had dried and cracked on their faces, with moss and tiny sticks protruding. They looked like escapees from a horror film.

"What are you looking at?" Pap said.

"Nothing," Tully said, repressing a shudder. "Let's find out what's up ahead."

The sources of the roaring turned out to be a water slide, smooth rock slanting down a hundred feet or so at about the same angle as a slide Tully had once seen in a children's water park. A layer of green moss covered the rock with water flowing over the top. The slide ended in a scoop of sorts above a long deep pool of water. A fisherman stood whipping his line out over the pool. He seemed about the size of an ant.

Pap gasped out a limp profanity. Under other circumstances, Pap would have been ashamed of its feebleness, Tully thought.

"I ain't going down that!" Pap said.

Tully looked at the canyon walls closing in on each side. Then he turned and looked back the way they had come. "We either have to go back through the devil's clubs and the blowdown or do the slide. It's impossible to make our way around the cliffs."

Dave studied the slide. "It looks doable. The pool of water down below looks deep enough to cushion the landing once you get shot out of that scoop thing."

Pap heaved a sigh. "So it all ends like this."

"Don't be such a pessimist," Tully said. "This actually could be fun. It's even better than some of those Disneyland water rides, like the one where you come down the chute in a hollow log."

"I hate that one!" Pap said. "And this slide is ten times bigger! And there could be sharp rocks caught in the moss. Just imagine your rear end going over one of those rocks!"

Tully said, "Well, just imagine fighting your way through those devil's clubs and climbing back up over the blowdown from the bottom side. Anyway, you don't have to be the first, Pap. If Dave runs into any serious trouble on the way down, we can figure out what we want to do then."

Dave had been scrutinizing the slide. He turned around. "What was that? I'm not going down first! No, our fearless leader is going first! That's you, Bo!"

"Actually, I would, Dave, but I thought I should stay behind to look after my old father, while you see how safe the slide is."

Dave looked at Pap. "You know what, Bo, we could both grab Pap and throw him onto the slide and see how he makes out."

"Sounds like a good plan," Tully said.

"Ain't gonna happen," Pap said. "You're going to have a hard time throwing an armed man onto that slide."

Tully took another look at the slide. "Oh, all right, if both of you are too chicken, I'll go first. Help me find a couple of short sticks to use as brakes. I'll drag them along through the moss to slow me down."

Dave waded over to the bank and snapped off a couple of foot-long pieces from a driftwood branch. He gave them to Tully, who was once again studying the slide. "You think these will work as brakes, Bo?"

"It's pretty clever, if I do say so myself." He put a stick in each hand.

"Well, shove off, Bo," Pap said. "We ain't got all day."

"Shut up! I'm still studying the situation. Hey, down there!" he yelled at the fisherman. The man didn't look up.

Pap said, "The water's too loud. He can't hear you." He put a foot in the middle of his son's back and gave a push. Tully never had a chance to use either brake. Pap said later he had the impression Bo had shot out from under his hat, which floated in the air for a second like a cartoon hat, then followed its owner. Tully streaked down the slide flat on his back, the two brakes held in the air. He briefly worried about the chute at the bottom, but then he was flying through the air. He landed in a splash halfway down the pool. He grabbed his hat and paddled over to a slab of rock at the edge of the water and pulled himself out. The clay was dripping down his face. He swept back his hair and looked around for the fisherman. The man was gone. His fly rod was lying on the rock.

Tully couldn't understand how the man had disappeared so quickly. He peered up at the two tiny figures at the top of the slide. At least I'm not up there, he thought. Sitting down on the slide had given him the worst feeling he had ever had in his life.

Dave streaked down next, holding Pap's gold pan against his chest. He turned a complete somersault after leaving the chute and splashed down in the pool. Sputtering, he came to the surface, turned over on his back, and kicked to the rock ledge. Then Pap came flying through the air and splashed into the pool. He swam over to Tully's rock and looked up at him. Tully looked down. "There, that wasn't so bad, was it, Pap?"

Pap said, "I've had a lot of terrible things forced on me, but this is the first time I ever had to choose something that awful for myself."

"Me, too," Tully said. "It's having to think about doing it beforehand that makes it so terrible."

"Tell me about it!" Dave said, whitened fingers still clasping Pap's gold pan to his chest.

14

They left the fisherman's fly rod where it lay and worked their way around the lower pool. They came to a flattened area. The side of the canyon above them was covered with a slope of broken rock, but the ground next to the creek was carpeted with a patch of green moss. Tully looked at his watch. It was nearly noon. He took a metal flask of whiskey and a lunch of elk sausages wrapped in pancakes out of his belly pack. They sat down on a log next to the creek and ate in silence. After lunch, Pap tried his gold pan on some sand he scraped out of a crack in a large rock. Tully and Dave lay in the sun and watched him. "Hey, we're rich!" Pap yelled.

Dave and Tully wandered over to look at the treasure. Pap stuck his index finger down at the edge of a line of black sand and held the tip up for them to see two tiny specks of gold.

"How many of those do we need for a troy ounce?" Dave asked.

"About a hundred billion," Pap said. "It does show there's gold here, though. Might have been a lot more at one time, but like I said, these cricks get worked pretty hard by guys with portable gold dredges."

Pap took a deep drag of whiskey from the flask. "Man, that warms me up inside and out. Now that I feel almost alive again, this looks kind of like the place I should take a nap." He walked over to a sunny spot away from the creek and lay down on his back.

Dave looked up at the mass of broken rock that had slid down the mountain. "I used to know what they called a slide of rocks like that," he said, pointing.

"A scree," Pap said.

"That's it, a scree. I guess it all came loose from that cliff up there. Water gets in a crack and freezes and breaks the rock loose and in a few thousand years you got yourself a scree."

Pap thrashed around on the ground. "Of all the places I find to take a nap, I have to find the one with a pointy rock on it. He sat up and started to scrape away at the dirt. "Well, I'll be darned. Lookee here what I found." He held up the rusted head of a pick.

Tully and Dave walked over to look at the find. It was covered with rust but still contained a piece of the rotted handle. They both turned and looked up at the steep rocky slope above them. "Nothing up there," Dave said. "Like a mine."

"Doesn't appear to be," Tully said. "Maybe I'll climb up a ways and have a look around."

"Be my guest," Dave said, lying down alongside Pap. "Maybe I'll have a nap myself."

Tully worked his way carefully up the scree. The rocks were loose and shifted under his feet, a sign they hadn't been walked on much, not that there was any reason at all for them to be walked on. He climbed back down. Dave glanced up at him from the ground.

"Find anything?"

"No. Oh, I did find a rock with a perfectly round hole in it. It was too heavy to carry back here though."

Pap sat up. "That's got to be a drill hole. Maybe this scree didn't just tumble down naturally over a million years. Maybe it was blasted loose from that cliff up there!"

They sat in silence for several moments. "The question is," Pap finally said, "why would anyone want to blast all this rock loose for no reason at all? It's totally use-less."

"Unless it was intended to hide some-thing," Dave said.

"Like the entrance to a mine," Tully added.

Dave studied the scree and then looked at the water slide. "Say, Bo, hand me that picture Agatha gave you of Sean O'Boyle."

Tully unwrapped the plastic and handed him the photo. Dave turned and held the picture out at arm's length. "You know what that white stuff in the picture is?"

"Don't have a clue."

"It's the water slide."

15

They rolled rocks down the mountain for the rest of the day without finding what they were looking for, namely the opening to a mine. Then they climbed to the top of the scree and worked their way around the cliff. Tully had worried they would run into another blowdown, but the slope above the scree was sparsely covered with trees and relatively easygoing. They came up right at the Finch Mine and Tully's truck.

They drove into Angst and rented a motel room. Tully washed and dried clothes at a Laundromat while Pap and Dave waited on a bench looking at months-old copies of *People* magazine. Then they took the clean clothes back to the motel and went over to Jake's Café for dinner. Stubb and Gordy were sitting at their favorite table with two other loggers. Tully held up his hands. "No need to get up, fellas," he said. "We can find a table in back."

One of the other loggers said, "What was that all about?"

"Nothing," said Gordy. "Just some guy smarting off."

Bev came to take their orders. "You guys!" she said. "Welcome back!"

"Nice to see you again, Bev," Dave said. "What's good tonight?"

"I'm pushing the Canadian stew," she said. "It ain't good, but it's the best we have."

"Sounds delicious," Tully said.

The four loggers, or whatever they were, got up and left. "Glad to see them go," Tully said. "When you got assaulted the other day, Dave, I was about ready to flash my badge. That would have put them in their place."

"Thanks a lot, Bo. It's always nice to have someone rush to my rescue."

"Where did you learn those moves anyway?" Pap asked.

"You promise not to tell?"

"Yup."

"Right. Well, I'll tell you anyway. I spent a year in Japan once. I didn't have a whole lot to do, so I signed up for a martial arts course run by these polite little Japanese gentlemen in cute white outfits who didn't in the least appear to be evil aliens from outer space. Because of their training, Pap,

I could break both your arms in four places in three seconds, should you give me reason. So don't give me any."

"Three seconds?" Pap said. "I'm pretty slow now that I'm old, but it used to take me only three seconds to be half a block away. I've always found fleeing to be the best defense."

"I come from a family of warriors," Tully said.

"To tell the truth, I kind of like the idea of fleeing myself," Dave said. "Those little guys beat me until I couldn't crawl, let alone flee. And then they charged me big time for all the pain they caused me."

"What were you doing in Japan anyway?" Tully asked. "Government work I bet."

"Afraid not. Strictly private enterprise."

Two men at a nearby table got up and headed for the door. They seemed to be having an argument. "You got to be kidding me!" one of them said. "You heard a loud screeching and then a monster came flying through the air and splashed into the pool you were fishing? Give me a break!"

"I'm not lying! The face on the thing was horrible!"

Pap and Dave watched the men leave and then turned to Tully.

"I don't recall any screeching," he said.

"What about the horrible face?"

"That kind of hurts my feelings."

The waitress brought their food.

"Wow," Pap said. "Looks like my favorite dish — Canadian stew!"

Bev laughed. "Next time you boys come in you can have Canadian hash. Jake changes the name on the stew whenever it's more than a week old."

Just then a young couple came through the front door, both of them wearing floppy sandals. Suddenly, the man grabbed the woman by the shoulders and tried to turn her back out the door. The woman said, "Bo, it's you!"

"Aha!" said Tully. "If it isn't my trusty deputy Ernie Thorpe and Miss Bunny Hunter!"

"It's like this, Bo," Ernie said. "Bunny — Miss Hunter — had to run a few errands in town, and I thought I'd better come along and protect her, in case Kincaid was around and like that."

"What about Agatha and Bernice?"

"What about them? Those are the toughest old ladies I've ever seen. They're armed to the teeth. If Kincaid should stop by, he won't be leaving, at least not under his own power. I take it he is still on the loose."

"He's up in the Snowies," Tully said.

"Anyway, join us for dinner. It's on the county."

"I recommend the Canadian stew," Dave said.

"Yeah," Tully said. "But by all means don't ever order the Canadian hash."

Bunny and Ernie sat down directly across from Tully, which improved his view enormously, at least in regard to Bunny. Several times she gave him a nice smile, for no reason at all, except maybe to let him know that Ernie wasn't a serious entity. Pap got up and wandered back toward the kitchen. Bev came rushing out, and he squeezed some bills into her hand. Before she could protest, he returned to the table. Tully nodded at him and gave him a smile. That's when he felt a foot slip up the bottom of his pant leg and rub up and down on his leg. Bunny was looking at Ernie, pretending to be interested in some stupid story he was telling. Tully, Dave, and Pap finished their after-dinner beers and reluctantly, at least for Tully, headed back to the truck.

Driving to the mine, Tully couldn't help but smile. He still had it. Why he ever thought an oaf like Ernie could beat him out with Bunny, he'd never know.

"Why you smiling, Bo?" Pap asked.

"No reason."

"Good. I was hoping it wasn't because I ran my foot up your leg during dinner. Almost gave myself a cramp getting my boot off without you noticing."

Dave shouted, "Cripes, Bo! You almost ran us into the ditch!"

Pap cackled and started to roll himself a cigarette.

"You better roll a cigarette," Tully growled. "It could be your last. On second thought, I think I'll wait and kill you right after I kill Ernie Thorpe."

"Oh, if you're thinking of killing me, I'd better come clean," Pap said. "On my way back from the kitchen, I noticed Bunny slip off her sandal under the table. I figured she was up to no good. A minute later, I saw your eyes bug out and your face light up like a Christmas tree and Bunny was grinning like the Cheshire cat while she pretended she was listening to Ernie babble on."

"You better not be lying, Pap!"

"Cross my heart."

"And hope to die?"

"I don't think I'd go that far."

16

The next morning, Tully hated even the thought of rolling rocks for one more day. The fact they had found one drilled rock would keep him at it but not for much longer. There could be no reason for anyone blasting a cliff in this particular area, except to conceal something. "I'm losing all interest in Tom and the boy," he told Pap and Dave. "They'd both be dead by now anyway. So what's the point?"

"I'm getting a little short on curiosity myself," Dave said. He was peeling one of the oranges they had bought in Angst. Tully watched him. He thought the best part of oranges was the peeling of them. Dave said, "So, Bo, you come up with any idea about what we might be looking for?"

"Not a clue."

"Can't be a campsite," Pap said. "There are a lot easier ways to conceal a campsite than blowing up a cliff."

"We'll give it today," Tully said. "If we don't find something by five today, we'll go pick up the tent and head in."

"You're apparently not too worried about Kincaid," Dave said.

"No, he's had his shot and I'm getting so tired of roughing it I'd appreciate a little interruption by old Lucas. It's pretty inconsiderate of him to leave us alone for so long. I'm much more concerned about Brian."

"Yeah," Pap said. "I'm surprised you would put him up against Kincaid."

"He's the best I have," Tully said.

"Ain't good enough."

They went back to rolling rocks. Then Dave found a hollow under one of them. Smaller rocks slid down and vanished through a tiny hole. The hole grew bigger. A few minutes later, he uncovered a sharp edge of rock with an opening below it.

"It's the mine!"

Tully scrambled across the scree and looked at the opening. "Tom and Sean's mine!" he shouted. "Has to be! It looks more like a rabbit hole, though. Can't be more than three feet from bottom to top."

Pap said, "If you want to hide it, maybe under a pile of sticks, a small entrance makes it a lot easier."

Dave took out his handkerchief and

mopped sweat from his forehead. "I think you're right about that. If we clear a few more rocks away, we should be able to drop down in front of it."

"I ain't going down in there without a flashlight," Pap said. "A hardhat wouldn't be a bad idea, either."

"I don't have any hardhats," Tully said, "but I've got some flashlights in the truck and a lantern. There's a good rope there, too. I'll climb up and get them."

"Don't bother with the lantern," Pap said. "Going into an old mine with a flame of any kind ain't a good idea."

Dave said, "I don't think going into any old mine at all is a good idea."

"Probably not," Pap said.

Tully was already climbing up the scree toward the cliff. He was happy once again the blowdown hadn't reached this far down the drainage. Before gathering up the rope and flashlights, he leaned his head against the truck canopy and gasped for breath. He hadn't felt this excited in a long time. It felt good, but he didn't want to kill himself. He was on the ultimate treasure hunt, this time for an actual gold mine. Going back down the scree he angled over a ways so as not to send an avalanche down on Pap and Dave. He could see Pap sitting on the rocks above the mine opening. He was smoking one of his hand-rolleds. Dave was climbing back up the scree from the creek, a small log over his shoulder. He threw it down on the rocks. Coming down to them, Tully said, "Glad to see you're both hard at work. What's the log for, Dave?"

"We're going to need something to tie the rope to, Bo, unless you know one of those Indian rope tricks where it just stands by itself in the air."

"Well, let's see, an Indian rope trick would work as well as that log. We'd just pull it in after us."

"Dang! I wish I'd thought of that!" Dave said. "On the other hand, maybe we can tie on the rope and then pile rocks on the log. Do you suppose that might work, Bo?"

Tully smiled. "Might work." He handed each of them a flashlight and then tied the rope to the center of the log. He laid the log a few feet from the opening, which Pap and Dave had enlarged in the scree. They piled enough rocks on the log to hold an elephant, as Pap pointed out.

"Okay," Tully said, "which one of you wants to go first?"

"Pap's smallest," Dave said. "I vote for him."

"And the most expendable," Tully said.

"He's got my vote, too."

Pap responded with an obscenity. "If you guys are too chicken, I'm happy to go first. Never have been able to stand the company of pantywaists."

"What's a pantywaist, anyway?" Dave said.

"Beats me," Tully said. "It doesn't make any sense."

Pap took the rope, wrapped it around his shoulder and back between his legs, and began walking his way down through the scree. Dave and Tully peered down at him from the edge. He reached bottom, knelt down, took a flashlight from his pocket, and directed the beam into the entrance hole.

"See anything?" Dave shouted down.

Pap looked up. "The only way I can see anything is to get down on my hands and knees and crawl through the hole. And stop shouting! I suspect if there's any support timbers down here they are pretty well rotted. The hum of a mosquito could bring the whole thing down."

Dave looked at Tully. "You're next."

"Thanks." Tully grabbed the rope and slowly worked his way down through the scree to the hole. He noticed that he was standing on crushed rock, apparently tailings that had been excavated from the mine. He looked around. The mine was scarcely

more than a hole in the side of the mountain. Pap had already crawled inside. Tully
followed. Inside, the hole grew larger, but
the ceiling was barely high enough for him
to stand. At most, the mine was wide
enough for two men to walk abreast, if they
were both thin and excessively friendly.
Tully shined his flashlight down the tunnel.
A wooden wheelbarrow with a metal wheel
leaned against one wall. A dozen or so feet
beyond it, the mine curved to the left. "Find
anything?" he whispered to Pap.

"Just a bunch of rags over there," Pap
whispered back, pointing to a row of rags at
the edge of the tunnel.

"Let's wait for Dave. I see what you mean
about rotted timbers. There aren't that
many timbers to begin with. I guess Tom
and Sean weren't too concerned about such
niceties."

Dave came down. "Glad you waited for
me."

"Whisper!" Pap whispered. He pointed at
an overhead timber.

Dave looked at the timber and then back
at the entrance hole. "It might be a good
idea for one of us to wait topside, in case
there's a cave-in or something. I volunteer."

"That's not a bad idea," Tully whispered.
"We'll let Pap do it, though."

"But I wanted to see the rest of the mine," Pap said.

"You can see it later. We need somebody up top."

Grumbling, Pap got down on his hands and knees and crawled back out of the mine.

"How come you picked me to stay instead of Pap?" Dave said. "He's the one who knows something about mines, although this appears to be nothing but a narrow tunnel blasted through solid rock."

"Because Pap isn't scared enough. He's liable to strike a match and light one of his hand-rolleds. There could be a box of dynamite rotting away down here all these years. Maybe all the nitroglycerine would have evaporated or whatever nitroglycerine does when it oozes out of dynamite. I don't want to take any chances."

"Well, I'm scared enough, Bo. You don't have to worry about me."

They worked their way back into the mine, Tully sweeping the beam from his flashlight back and forth ahead of them. The mine seemed surprisingly dry, but odd smells drifted in the stale air, none of them pleasant. Dave held his finger to his nose, as if he were about to sneeze. Wide-eyed, Tully glared at him and pointed to the ceiling. The sneeze went away. Tully sighed in relief.

Various rusted tools leaned against the walls. They came to an open wooden box, the dynamite inside having deteriorated into a spongy mass. Tully pointed to it and shook his head. Dave rolled his eyes.

The mine ended at a wall of white quartz. Tully shined his flashlight on it. He spit on his hand, wiped a spot clean, and examined it closely. The wall was threaded with veins of gold. Tom and Sean had hit it big. He motioned toward the quartz. Dave mouthed, "Wow!"

"Hey, looked at this," Tully whispered, pointing to a long-handled sledgehammer and a set of chisel-bit steel drilling rods lined up neatly against the wall. "Tom and Sean intended to return to work. No miner would ever leave behind a set of steel drills, let alone the gold. I think we're looking at a double-jack setup."

"What's a double jack?"

"It's two guys, the miner and a helper, in this case Tom and Sean. The miner got a person with a low IQ to hold the steel while the miner hit it with the long-handled sledge. I suspect O'Boyle was the fellow with the low IQ. A single jack was basically a one-man drill. He held the drill bit with one hand and hit it with a short-handled sledge in the other hand."

"Sounds labor-intensive."

"No kidding! After the smart guy in the double jack hit the drill bit with the big sledge, the dumb guy gave the steel a quarter turn and the bit chipped out about a quarter inch of rock. Once the hole got too deep for the first steel, they replaced it with the next longer one and so on. To get a blasting hole deep enough, I've heard it took a hundred swings of the sledge."

"Let's get out of here," Dave said. "This place is too spooky for me."

"We haven't found any bodies. I don't know if that's bad or good."

"It's just that I don't ever want to get so close to that much work."

"Me, neither."

They made their way back to the opening. Dave got down on his knees and crawled out. He grabbed the rope and started working his way up through the scree. While he waited, Tully picked up a stick and poked around in the rags at the edge of the mine. Then he climbed out.

"No bodies, huh?" Pap said.

"A box of dynamite," Dave said. "And a double-jack setup and other tools."

"And two skeletons," Tully said.

"Skeletons?"

"Yeah, Dave, those rags along the edge of

the mine, they were clothes with two skeletons underneath."

Dave ran his hand back through his hair as if clearing something from his mind. "Somebody blasted rocks down over the mine and trapped them in there," he said. "What a miserable way to die!"

"No way is good as far as I'm concerned," Pap said.

Dave said, "So you think somebody blew the mine shut and left them in there to die?"

"I've been thinking about that. I can't imagine Tom and Sean wouldn't have noticed somebody drilling up above them on the cliff. Also, I don't think they would just have lain down together and waited to die. I'm going to call my Crime Scene Investigations Unit and get it up here to see what it can figure out."

Dave looked puzzled for a moment. "Oh, yeah, I forgot. Your CSI unit consists of only one guy."

"Lurch is good, too," Pap said. "Solves most of Bo's crimes for him."

"I wouldn't say most," Tully said. "But he's pretty good."

Tully took out his cell phone and dialed Daisy.

"Hi, Daisy. It's Bo, and I — !"

"Bo! About time you called in! I — We

163

have been worried sick about you!"

"You could have called me if you were so concerned!"

"You may remember telling me never to call unless there's an emergency I can't handle!"

Tully winked at Dave. "Oh, good. So there hasn't been an emergency. I've been gone less than a week and no emergency. That must be a record."

"There have been emergencies, but nothing I couldn't handle!" Daisy said. "I've been spending night and day with your mom, and I think she's getting pretty sick of me."

"It's okay for you to get back to the office and do some work. You can sleep at home, too."

"The Kincaid business is over?"

"I'll tell you about it later. I should be back in a couple of days. Do you know where Lurch is?"

"Yeah, he's at the office. I just talked to him."

"Thanks." He dialed Lurch's number.

"Hi," Lurch said. "How's it going, boss?" Apparently nobody but Tully ever called the unit.

"It just got interesting, Lurch. I need you up here pronto. Bring your kit and throw in

a metal detector. I've got a couple of skeletons in pretty bad shape, and I want you
to figure out what caused them to become
skeletons. Bring something to haul them
back in."

Tully told him how to get to the Finch
Mine. Lurch said he would meet them at
the mine's chain in two hours.

17

Tully drove down to the chain to wait for Lurch, but the unit was already there. They drove their vehicles back up to the Finch Mine and unloaded two plastic cases from Lurch's Explorer. Lurch said they would be used to put the bones in. He would take them back to Blight for more careful analysis.

Lurch pointed to the various structures of the Finch Mine. "It looks kind of creepy. Like all the workers disappeared yesterday, but it's been shut down sixty years or so, right?"

"Right," Tully said. "It's like it has been frozen in time."

They put one plastic box in the other and Lurch's gear in that one and hauled it down the scree, Tully carrying the front end of the boxes, Lurch the back. Wearing only oxfords, the CSI unit wasn't happy about having to tramp down the steep grade on loose rocks. Going down the hole on a rope made him even more unhappy. "I don't like the looks of this!" he yelled up from the bottom.

Tully came down on the rope. He pointed at the small opening into the mine and gestured for Lurch to crawl through. The unit shook its head.

"Oh, all right," Tully said. "If you're going to turn chicken on me, Lurch, I'll go first. Remember, once we're inside talk only in a whisper."

"Oh, great," Lurch said.

Pap and Dave lowered the CSI kit and first plastic case down with the rope. Tully reached out and pulled the first one into the mine. He gave the rope a tug. Pap or Dave pulled it back up and the second case came down. Then the unit.

Tully pointed at the rags. "That's where the skeletons are."

Lurch took two pairs of latex gloves from his kit and handed one pair to Tully.

"I don't need gloves," Tully whispered, "because I ain't touching anything! I'm just here to hold the flashlight."

"Yes, you're touching!" Lurch whispered, snapping on his own gloves. "I'm going to need your help to lift the skeletons into the cases, if we want to get them out of here in any shape resembling the original."

It soon became evident that the skeletons would make it into the cases in several pieces. Lurch picked up a gray skull and examined it. "This guy was pretty young. The teeth are perfect. He picked up the other skull. "Ditto here. Not much chance of getting a definite ID. Like none at all." He turned the second skull over in his hands.

"There are two belt buckles here," Tully said. He held them up. "What about those?"

"They're pretty fancy," Lurch said. "Big fancy buckles. They must have been cowboys."

"Kind of, I suppose. What I was thinking, Agatha has photographs of the two of them. Maybe we can use a magnifying glass to check their belt buckles in the photos."

"Good idea! Might work. I can tell you one thing right now about how they were killed."

"So tell me, Lurch."

"They were both shot in the back of the head. They were both lying facedown with their hands tied behind them and their feet tied together. They were executed with shots to the head. Pretty terrible, if you ask me. Why tie them up? Why not just shoot them?"

"Whoever did it probably didn't think that

far ahead. After he had them tied up, he couldn't figure out what to do with them. Maybe he thought the kind thing to do was shoot them. So he shot them. You know, Lurch, it's possible these bones don't belong to Agatha's father or the O'Boyle boy. Maybe we'll just give them to the family and say that's who the bones belong to. How could they tell? It will give them something to bury, anyway."

"Gee, I don't know about that."

"Don't get picky on me now, Lurch. Besides, maybe we'll get IDs from the buckles."

"Yeah, I'd prefer that to the Blight Way. So are we done here?"

"Not quite," Tully said. He walked over to the entrance hole, knelt down, and stuck his head out. In a loud whisper, he said, "Pap, send down the metal detector." A few minutes later the metal detector came down on the rope.

"Ah," said Lurch. "You want to look for the bullets."

"Actually, I want *you* to look for the bullets. I myself try to avoid learning how to operate any machine I don't have to. If you're right that Tom and Sean were shot right here while lying facedown, the bullets have to be here someplace."

Lurch clicked on the metal detector and began sweeping it back and forth over the rubble. Almost immediately, the instrument began to beep. He took out a flat wooden stick and began to dig down through the rocks. Picking up a small object, he blew it off. Tully leaned over his shoulder to get a better look.

"What is it, Lurch?"

"Just what you wanted — one of the bullets that killed our vics here."

"Not likely there would be any other bullet right at this spot. Can you make out any striations on it?"

Lurch spit on the object and wiped it off. "Yeah, enough to identify the gun it was fired out of. Here's something weird. It's green! Good luck finding that gun, after, what, about eighty years?"

Tully squinted at the bullet. "Spit on it again, Lurch, and see if you can identify the caliber. I'm always amazed by your advanced technology."

"Weird," Lurch said. "You ever heard of a green bullet, Bo?"

"Yeah, half my bullets are green. They get old and wet, the brass turns green. This one has to be brass-covered. What kind of weapon fires it?"

"Don't know. I'll have to check it out back

at my lab."

"You don't have a lab."

"I just say that to fool people. I do have some resources available to me, though, stuff I've scrounged, stolen, and bought with my own pitiful earnings."

"If you're done whining, Lurch, let's get out of here. This place gives me the creeps."

They sent the cases with the two skeletons up on the rope, and followed them with the CSI kit. Then Lurch climbed out. Tully took what he hoped would be a last look at the mine. He hated to leave gold behind, but he knew the tunnel would have to be blasted shut for good. One stick of dynamite would bring the whole thing down. He probably could get Buck Toole to light the fuse and then scramble up through the scree. As he liked to say, there was always use for dumb in law enforcement.

18

Lurch took the skeletons and bullets back to Blight. Tully, Pap, and Dave drove to the Quail Creek Ranch. Agatha and Bernice came out to greet them. "Any luck?" Agatha asked.

"We found the remains of a couple of victims," Tully said. "I think they probably belong to Tom and the O'Boyle boy. They were right in the range we guessed at from judging the time and gait of the horses. In any case, they were murdered, just as you suspected. All we have that might identify them is a couple of belt buckles. I know you have photos of the two of them. If we can make out the belt buckles in the pictures, that's as close as we can come to IDs."

Bernice gave Agatha a hug and then she came over and gave Tully a kiss on the cheek. "I knew you could do it, Bo!"

Ernie Thorpe and Bunny came out of the house. What were the two of them doing in there unsupervised? Tully thought.

"Oh, Bo!" cried Bunny. "Did you solve the mystery for Aunt Agatha?"

"Solved part of it, I think. Haven't pinned down the murderer yet."

Agatha said, "I want to bury the remains right here on the ranch, Bo. Can we do that?"

"I'm sure it can be arranged, if they happen to be your dad's."

"Even if they aren't, I'd like to bury them here!"

"Fine with me," Tully said. "What about the O'Boyle boy, if the remains turn out to be his?"

"I don't know of any O'Boyles who live around here anymore. If you can't find any family who want him, we'll take Sean, too, right, Bernice?"

"Right, Agatha. We'll find beautiful resting places for both of them. I'll weld each of them up a nice marker, too."

Pap said, "If everybody is done yakking, let's go see if we can identify the two of them from a photo. Also, I'd be interested to know if you have a beer lurking around your refrigerator, Agatha."

"I've been expecting you back at any time, Pap. Of course I have a beer waiting for you. A whole case, if you want it."

"That sounds about right. I been dying of thirst ever since Bo drug me off on this adventure."

They all went in the house. Agatha turned on the light over the dining-room table and dug out two well-worn photo albums. She placed them on the table. Tully laid the two belt buckles side by side next to the albums. Agatha stared at them for a moment, as if thinking about the last time they had been buckled. Then she started flipping through pages of the album. She came to an old brown photo with cracks spiderwebbed across it. It showed a bearded young man standing next to a teenage boy with long, light-colored hair. The man wore a floppy hat and had a pick over his shoulder. The boy leaned on a shovel. Both of them were grinning at the camera.

"Bernice, get me the magnifying glass, please," Agatha said.

Bernice went into another room and came back with the glass. "I don't know why," she said, "but I'm shaking all over."

Agatha held the glass up to the photo. Tully leaned over Agatha's shoulder. "It's a match! The buckle on the left belongs to Tom. The one on the right belongs to Sean! We've got them back!"

Agatha wiped a tear from her cheek.

Bernice turned abruptly and walked away. "Oh, Bo, I am so happy!" Agatha cried. "After all this time, you've found them. Nobody except Bernice and me believed you could do it."

Pap said, "I didn't believe it myself. Now, Agatha, are you going to get me that beer or do I have to do it myself?"

"I'll get beer for everyone," Agatha said. "But everybody is going to have a shot of whiskey first. This is a celebration!"

"Sounds like my kind of celebration," Pap said. "For an old lady, you ain't too bad, Agatha."

Agatha made a harrumphing sound but couldn't help smiling broadly. She gave Pap a friendly pat on the shoulder as she went by.

After the celebration, Agatha and Bernice followed the three men back to their truck. Tully had told Ernie to stay at the ranch until he got back. Ernie pretended not to be happy as a lark.

Agatha said, "You think the trouble is over with Lucas Kincaid, Bo?"

"I doubt there's anything to worry about, but we're headed into Blight right now. We should be back in a couple of days. By the way, Agatha, Ernie, and Bunny seem to be getting along rather well."

"Yes, and I'm so happy. You know, Bunny has been married twice already, and it didn't take either time."

"Twice?" Tully said.

"Yes. I don't know what the problem is, but Bunny is something of a perfectionist. That could have something to do with it."

"A perfectionist," Tully said. "I don't know a lot of perfect men. Other than me, I can't think of even one."

"What about Ernie?" Agatha asked. "He's such a nice young man. And so nice looking, too!"

"Oh, yeah," Tully said begrudgingly. "Ernie is okay."

"And he has an actual job! That's something these days!"

"You're right about that, Agatha."

Tully, Dave, and Pap spent the night in a motel and had breakfast at the House of Fry the next morning. Tully and Pap then drove over to Batim Scragg's to check on Clarence. The old man and the dog were out in the front yard. Batim was throwing a ball for Clarence and Clarence was chasing it.

"That is so disgusting," Pap said.

"Yeah," Tully said. "I certainly wouldn't have expected it of Batim."

"I meant Clarence. He made a career of

176

biting old ladies on the ankles but at least he had some dignity."

Batim walked over as Pap and Tully got out of the pickup. Clarence followed him, carrying the ball and wagging his tail.

"You two seem to be hitting it off," Tully said.

"I tell you, Bo, this little guy is the best friend I ever had. Can't imagine how you ever thought to give him to me."

"Like I said, two peas in a pod."

"You was sure right about that. By the way, Lucas Kincaid stopped by again, not long after you was here. He got hisself a nice new Humvee."

"Must have struck it rich, Batim."

"Must of stole it, I figured. I did think about killing him for you, Bo, but he was kind of wary and it didn't seem worth the try. I did let slip that you was going to the campsite up on Deadman. You didn't let on like it was a secret of any kind, and I figured you know how to take care of yourself."

"No problem, Batim. I wasn't making any secret of it. I always feel I can keep one step ahead of the bad guys. Otherwise, I'd give up sheriffing."

"That's what I figured, Bo. I didn't want to cause you any problems."

"No, you did just fine. Mostly I wanted to

177

see how you and Clarence were getting along."

"Oh, we're doing great, Bo."

"Glad to hear it, Batim."

Tully and Pap got back in the truck and headed toward Blight City. Pap rolled himself another cigarette, pulled the string on the bag of Bull Durham tight with his teeth, licked the edge of the paper, sealed the crooked little cigarette shut, and punched in the lighter.

"How many years you been making those hand-rolleds, Pap?"

"Since I was about eight. You do the math, Bo."

"I was just wondering how come with all that practice your cigarettes still turn out crooked as a snake."

" 'Cause I like them like that. What do you care anyway?"

"Just curious. Seems to me that after seventy-some years you would get practiced up."

"I'll tell you something *I'm* curious about, Bo. How come you let that Susan get away? I thought she was a little fancy for you and way too educated but she's mighty beautiful."

"I like her, too. But she found herself an airline pilot she liked better than me. He was handsome and made a lot of money and owned a big ranch and flew all over the world and his family and girlfriends could fly free all over the world too, but despite all that, she still liked him better than me. A man just can't figure women anymore. Airline pilots are like a plague of locusts. They swoop down and glom up every good-looking woman in sight."

Pap grabbed the lighter and lit his cigarette. As was his practice, he blew the first plume of smoke in Tully's face. "The one thing I didn't like about Susan was her occupation."

"Medical examiner?"

"Yeah," Pap said. "You never wanted to ask Susan what she did that day. That murder victim we found hanging over Batim's fence, you see her take the body's temperature?"

"No! I shut my eyes first!"

"I mightily regret I didn't have the good sense to do that. Other than her job, though, I can't think of another drawback. I'd take another run at her if I was you, Bo."

"You think so?"

"Can't hurt."

"You're wrong about that."

19

Tully walked into the office, his three-thousand-dollar boots *clok*ing nicely on the marble-chip floor. Herb Elliot was back to sitting on the edge of Daisy's desk, chatting her up. Daisy was laughing! Didn't Herb realize that Daisy was now divorced? The man was a fool!

"Bo!" Daisy yelled. "You're back! I was so worried about you!" She leaped up and gave him a hug.

Herb stuck out his hand. "Glad you're back safe and sound."

Tully gave his hand a couple of shakes. "You two held down the fort, I take it. At least I didn't get any panicky phone calls from Daisy."

"Daisy and I kept the department running like a fine-tuned engine," Herb said.

"Solve any crimes?"

"Naw, we worked mostly on fine-tuning. Oh, we got one nut running around holding up convenience stores every night at eight o'clock. The newspaper and radio have started calling him the 'Eight O'clock Robber.' "

"Probably just what he needs, a little publicity."

"We got the convenience stores staked out. There are twelve in all. We're trying to outguess him, but he's been beating us. He hasn't hurt anybody."

"Yet!" said Tully. "Sooner or later these jokers blow somebody up. Or somebody blows them up."

"So what about Kincaid?" Daisy asked. "You kill him, Bo?"

"Afraid not. Any word from Pugh, by the way?"

Daisy said, "No, not since he checked out that murder scene up at Woods Lake. I thought he was joining up with you."

"Yeah, I've got him busy. I thought he might have called in though."

Daisy gave him a puzzled look and shook her head.

Herb said, "Lurch tells us you've pretty much solved those old murders up in Angst."

"Part of it anyway. At least we know it was murder and who was murdered. We don't know who did the murder, though. It's a picky thing, but you can't count a murder solved until you've found the murderer."

"He would be dead now anyway," Herb said.

"Yeah, that's the problem. And that's the problem with the death penalty, too. The murderer gets the same sentence as everybody else in the world. We're all under a death sentence, same as a guy who murders ten people."

"There's a thought to cheer my day," Daisy said.

"Gee, I never thought of it that way," Herb said.

"I expect not, Herb. Anyway, we're going to hold a little burial service up at Quail Creek Ranch for Tom Link and the O'Boyle boy. I guess there'll be only six or seven of us there, which is kind of sad. Their lives were cut off just as they were about to become rich. Anyway, I've got to make a phone call." He walked into his office.

Daisy called after him. "You need me?"

"Remains to be seen." Tully closed the door.

He dialed Susan's work number. She answered. "Bo! You're back!"

"Yeah, just made it in. Hope I'm taking you away from some of your work."

"Actually, you are. I'm doing that nice old

182

couple from Woods Lake. Apparently, it's the work of your friend Kincaid."

"How do you know they were nice?"

"They're nice now. Death improves a person's character enormously."

Tully started doodling a cartoon of Susan on his desk calendar. He put little horns on the side of her head. "You're starting to sound like me. Anyway, I was just wondering how you and the flyboy are getting along, Susan."

"You interested in him, Bo?"

"Not unless he can get me free airline tickets."

"Well, he's history."

"You broke up with him!"

"Yes."

Tully scribbled in some dark hair that covered up the horns.

"Does this mean I still have a chance?"

"Bo, the only reason I broke up with you is that you're rude, crude, obnoxious, arrogant, egotistical, inattentive, insensitive, inane, and gross."

"I'm not inane! So how about dinner at Crabbs tonight?"

"I'd love to! I thought you'd never call. Why I ever gave you up for a jerk of an airline pilot, I'll never know."

"Free flights, all over the world." Tully

183

gave the cartoon big eyes with long curling lashes.

"Well sure, there's that," Susan said. "Let me think about this. No, we're still on for dinner."

"Great!" He gave the cartoon a tiny nose and a big beaming smile.

He hung up and opened his door. "Get in here, sweetheart," he yelled at Daisy. "I've got a bunch of things I want you to take care of."

Daisy bustled in, her high heels clicking smartly on the floor. She sat down in a chair across from him, all business now, her back ramrod straight.

Tully said, "First thing is, find Judge Patterson and get me a search warrant for Mr. Teddy Finch's home up in Angst."

"What's Finch's address?"

"How should I know? Find it. Where's Lurch?"

"Probably home sleeping. He's hardly slept since he got back."

"Call him up and tell him to get his butt down here. I want those bullets from the mine identified right now."

"Right."

"See if you can get ahold of Pugh and tell him he's got two weeks off. I've had him working night and day for the past month."

Daisy frowned. "Two weeks?"

"Oh, right, one week is enough."

"I don't know how to get ahold of Brian. We haven't heard from him and haven't been able to reach him. He must have his cell phone turned off. I thought you knew where he was."

"You mean he isn't back?"

"Back from where? You're the only one who knows what he's up to."

Tully stared at the wall behind Daisy.

"What's wrong, Bo?"

"Nothing. If you hear from Brian, you call me first thing, okay?"

"Okay. Why are you so upset?"

"I'm not upset. What were we talking about?"

Daisy rolled her eyes. "The search warrant. What shall I tell the judge you're searching for at the Finch place?"

"A gun."

"What kind of gun?"

"You're worse than our old judge! I need Lurch down here to find out what kind of gun!"

"Anything else?"

Tully tugged on the droopy corner of his mustache. "Yeah. Call up Ernie at Agatha's and tell him there's a red Humvee hidden back in the brush about half a mile south of

Deadman Creek. Have his friend Bunny drive him over there. Take the Humvee back to Agatha's. Keep everybody out of it, especially Bunny."

"Does Ernie have a key for it?"

Tully gave her The Look.

"Right. He'll know what to do if he hasn't."

Tully drove over to his mother's. The department mechanics had already replaced his window. The broken glass next to where his car had been parked a week before still littered the gutter. It made him think of Pugh again. Maybe he would give Brian two weeks off anyway. He went up the walk and pounded on the door.

"It's unlocked, Bo!" Rose shouted. "Come on in!"

"How did you know it was me, Ma?"

"You're the only one who almost knocks down the door." She came over and kissed him on the cheek. "Besides, Daisy called and told me to expect you. I guess she thought I might shoot you by mistake." She pointed to her .45 automatic on the table.

"I'm glad she called," Tully said. "So how did the two of you get along?"

"Oh, Daisy is such a lovely girl! But I'm afraid I was getting on her nerves."

"No, Ma! I can't imagine such a thing!"

"It's true, Bo. She did seem to enjoy my stories about you as a little boy."

"I was afraid of that. You didn't by any chance tell her about your own wild youth?"

"I may have mentioned one or two things, but Daisy found them amusing. She isn't one of those prissy women that irritate me so much."

"The ones with good taste?"

"Yes. Now tell me about Lucas Kincaid."

Tully sighed and slumped into an overstuffed chair with little white doilies on the arms. Rose frowned at him. He sat up straight.

"Not much to tell. Daisy won't be sleeping over here anymore, but you might want to keep your gun handy for a while. I'm back in town for tonight but have to get back up to Angst tomorrow. I'm putting the remains of a man and a boy in two coffins and hauling them up to Quail Creek Ranch for burial."

"Oh my. That is so awful. But it's good you found them. Is it legal to bury them on the ranch?"

He gave her his little smile, the one that said, do you really need to ask that question?

"Oh, right, I forgot, it's the Blight Way. I

hope you don't mind my mentioning it, Bo, but you look terrible. You better get to bed early tonight and get some sleep."

"Can't. I've got a date with Susan."

"Susan! Wonderful, Bo, wonderful! What happened to the airline pilot? You mean she's giving up the pilot for you?"

"What's so odd about that?"

"Nothing, dear, except for all those free flights."

Tully drove to his log house. Nothing had been broken into, and he was glad about that. The grass had started to grow back over the fire pits scattered about the meadow. Freezer Day was kind of a pain, but it beat campaigning. There wasn't a politician in all of Blight County who didn't wish he had thought of his own Freezer Day. The house was cold and empty. He turned off the double burglar alarms and looked around for something that seemed to be missing. Then he remembered — Clarence! He couldn't believe he had become attached to the little dog. Well, Batim could keep him. He remembered the shrimp man, too, Sid Brown and his Giggling Loon restaurant in Boise. He'd have to give the restaurant a try on his next trip to the big city. He remembered also Sid's mention of Jean Runyan, the art dealer, and that she wanted to give him a one-man show at the Davenport Hotel in Spokane. He was finally making enough money as an artist to give up his day job, his twenty-four-hour-a-day job. Maybe if the Bo Tully art show turned out well he would do just that.

The phone rang. Tully picked up. "Yeah?"

"It's me."

"Lurch! I've been looking for you. What have you found out about the bullets?"

"The closest I can come is the Spanish Reformado. It was a .43-caliber bullet used extensively in rolling-block rifles by the Cubans during the Spanish-American War. Because of the humidity in Cuba, the brass-coated bullets had a tendency to turn green. American troops thought the green made them poisonous. The bullets may have been poisonous, but because of all the germs in that moist climate. Anyway, over a million rounds of this ammo and a lot of the rolling-block rifles were captured by the American troops and brought back to the U.S. So it's possible one of them could have been in use here in 1927."

"Good work, Lurch. Now go back to bed."

"I'm awake now. I might as well go down to the office."

"That's even better."

Tully tried to remember something he had

heard about the Spanish-American War. Because it involved history, his mind had automatically shut off. Back in high school, a teacher might say, "Now, the ancient Greeks —" Tully's mind would instantly beep off.

He showered and shaved, trimmed his mustache, put on clean underwear, shirt, and pants, rubbed on a little aftershave, and then rummaged in his closet for a suitable jacket, finally settling on a black leather sport coat. He thought for a moment about switching his three-thousand-dollar-alligator-skin boots to a pair of oxblood loafers but then decided to stick with the boots. Susan was tall and the boots gave him a few more inches on her.

He watched the evening news on TV and then drove his sheriff's department Explorer into town. Susan was ready and looked fantastic and he complimented her on her frilly blue dress and gray jacket. He had decided to be particularly attentive for the evening. He would work on her other objections to his character later. One was about all he could manage for now.

"Crabbs, okay?" he said as they drove off.

"Sure," she said. "Best place to eat in Blight City."

"Yeah, and it's almost good, too. You ever

eaten at the Giggling Loon in Boise?"

"Yes, but I wasn't paying, fortunately."

"Pretty pricey, hunh?" Tully said, wondering who had picked up the tab.

"They don't bother to put the prices on the menu. I guess they figure if you want to know the prices you can't afford to eat there. Why, are you interested in taking me there sometime?"

"Maybe. As a matter of fact my paintings have been selling rather well lately. Jean Runyan has been thinking of giving me a one-man show up at the Davenport in Spokane. If that turns out well, I may just give up sheriffing."

"Oh, Bo, that would be wonderful! Being a successful artist is the best possible life a person can have. We could get us a big house on a beach off the coast of France! We could live anywhere! And we wouldn't have to drive your department Explorer when we go out to eat!"

"We?"

"Did I say we? Surely I meant you."

"I'm sticking with 'we.' "

Susan laughed. "I do think it would be a wonderful life."

Bo thought it was probably time for him to become attentive again. He glanced over at her but didn't detect anything to attend

191

to. This was harder than he expected. He thought of something but was afraid it might be interpreted as crude. Then he caught a whiff of her perfume. He decided to give it a shot. "Nice perfume."

"Why, thank you. I'm pleased you like it. You know, when you get to be a rich and famous artist you will be able to buy me perfume like this."

"That's something I'll have to learn," he said. "I've never been big on smells."

She stuck her face over close to him. "Depends on the smell," she said. "For example, I do detect you've just taken a shower and rubbed on some aftershave?"

"How do you like it?"

"The shower is wonderful."

Tully had called Crabbs earlier and talked to Lester Cline, the manager. He liked Lester well enough, even though he wasn't the sort of person Tully would want to go camping with. Tully described the table he and Susan had sat at a couple of times before. Lester had said he would hold it for them.

"I reserved our special table at Crabbs," he told her as they pulled into the restaurant's parking lot.

"Great!" Susan said. "Now tell me again exactly why this table is special?"

"We sat there twice before. Remember the last time, you were talking about your job and all the people at nearby tables moved away?"

"People can be so rude."

"Then you hooked up with the flyboy."

"That was a mistake," she said. "Maybe eating at Crabbs had something to do with it."

"Best place to eat in Blight City!"

"My point exactly."

Lester himself came out in a tuxedo and showed them to their special table. He had a white towel folded over his arm. "There you are, lady and gentleman," he said. "Now may I get you each a nice glass of wine?"

"By all means," said Tully. "Do you by any chance have Gallo White Merlot?"

"Oui, Monsieur, but here we call it Taste of Paris."

"Perfect. We'll have that. Okay with you, Susan?"

"One of my favorites," she said.

Trying to be attentive, he asked Susan what she had been up to lately.

"That grizzly double murder up at Woods Lake. It's one of the worst cases I've been on. I guess the worst part of it was —"

Tully raised his hand for her to stop. "Please, not when I'm about to eat."

"But it's so interesting!"

"I don't care."

"I understand from Daisy you don't mind picking up the bones of people who have been dead for nearly a hundred years."

Tully shook his head. "I do mind! Lurch made me do it! You will be impressed by this, however. We calculated roughly the distance between Quail Creek Ranch and the mine site by how fast horses walk and how fast humans walk."

"Very impressive," she said. "I assume your calculations turned out to be correct."

"Put us within a range of seven and a half miles."

"On Deadman Creek, I suppose. Everybody in town seemed to know you were staying at the campsite on Deadman."

Tully couldn't help but be highly attentive to her eyes. They may have been the biggest eyes he had ever seen on a woman. They were gorgeous, and also gave her a slightly startled look that added a certain cuteness to her beauty.

"That's what comes from being such a popular sheriff," he said. "Everybody wants to know where you're going and what you're doing."

"That's certainly true. Usually, though, it's not about camping."

The manager returned with their glasses of wine, followed by the waiter to take their orders.

"What's the special this evening?" Tully asked.

"Canadian stew," he said. "It's very good."

"I'll pass on that. What are you having, Susan?"

"The coconut shrimp. I love shrimp."

Tully studied the menu. "I've started liking shrimp a lot myself, ever since my Freezer Day. I'll go with the Captain's Plate. It's got lots of shrimp, right?"

"Yes, sir, it does."

Tully took a closer look at the waiter. "You look familiar. Have we met?"

"You arrested me for car theft a while back. I did a year."

"I have a terrible time keeping track of my criminals," Tully said. "Glad to see you've found fairly honest work. You haven't taken up poisoning or any hobbies like that, have you?"

The waiter laughed. "Actually, you were rather nice to me. You put together a fund for my wife and little girl while I was away."

"Really? Well, I appreciate your remembering. The name's Harvey Wilson, right?"

"Right."

Their meals and wine turned out to be

excellent, although Tully did wonder how one might go about poisoning shrimp. On the other hand, he thought, if Harvey poisons us, there goes his tip.

Tully passed on the dessert, but Susan went with the Suicide by Chocolate and devoured it with gusto. He would have to check out her hips to see if he could detect any spread. Actually, he had planned to check out her hips anyway, but Suicide by Chocolate gave him a good excuse. He wondered if that counted as attentive.

Susan said, "Bo, if we are going to proceed in a serious manner, I do have one favor to ask."

"Anything," he said.

"It's just that I'm bothered you have never gotten over Ginger. It's time you moved on. The large painting of her in the living room, the one where's she's holding the bouquet of wildflowers, you really should sell it."

Tully was silent. "Odd you should mention that painting," he said after a moment. "Sid Brown, the owner of the Giggling Loon, has offered to buy it. I could have my agent handle the deal."

"I hope you don't mind the advice," she said. "I'm usually pretty good at sizing up a situation. At least my usual clients never complain."

"I suppose not," he said.

"One other thing," Susan said. "I hate to bring it up, but must you wear those cowboy boots? You're not a cowboy, after all. Besides, I know you hate horses."

"It's my inner cowboy. He's the one who wears the boots. I'm the one that hates horses. Most of us old Idaho boys have inner cowboys. It doesn't make any difference what we do for a living. As a matter of fact, Susan, I really doubt you would have any interest in a man who didn't have an inner cowboy."

"Try me," she said.

After dinner, he dropped Susan off at her apartment. She claimed to be exhausted. He drove back to his lonely log house, wondering if Batim Scragg might be getting tired of Clarence by now. He wondered about Lucas Kincaid. In the pale light of the moon he scanned the tree line above his house, mostly out of habit. Lucas wasn't the only person with a hankering to kill him, should the opportunity arise. Keeping it from happening was second nature to Tully by now, and he kept himself most attentive in that regard. He hoped Daisy would have the search warrant in hand by the time he got to the office the next morning. He was getting bored with this whole business of

Agatha's mystery and was ready to move on
from that.

It was nearly six the next morning when he awoke. Nothing like a few murders to wear a person out. He got dressed, ate a bowl of Cheerios, and drove to the office.

"Where's Lurch?" he asked.

"On his way in," Daisy said. "He should be here any minute."

"I take it you were able to get all the info you needed for the warrant."

"Yeah, old Judge Patterson is pretty easy. You headed back up to Angst today?"

"Soon as Lurch shows up. Anything happening here?"

"Nothing I can't handle."

"That's what I figure," Tully said. "I got my own problems."

Daisy was particularly fetching in her black slacks and white blouse. Tully knew she was in love with him. People go through their whole lives with other people romantically in love with them and never know.

Tully knew. Daisy was a woman after all. He took his Picasso mug off the rack behind the coffee thermoses and managed to fizz out half a cup. The troops always seemed to run out the coffee before he arrived. He yelled at Florence. "Flo, would you make some more coffee, please? Daisy is too lazy to do it."

"You got it, boss. Take just a few minutes."

Daisy gave him a hard look. "I heard what you said to Florence. Lazy, my eye! I'm busy!"

"Busy, my eye. So how about the warrant?"

"I've got it right here. Judge Patterson wanted to know the time frame. I told him eighty-five years."

"Sounds about right. What did he say?"

"Nothing. You know he always gives you what you ask for."

"That's because he's the best kind of judge a cop can ask for, old and senile."

Daisy laughed. "And corrupt."

"Well, sure, but I've never paid him a dime. I think he's got me confused with Pap."

She gave him the warrant. He folded it up and slid it into the inside pocket of his sports coat.

Daisy said, "I see you're wearing your

three-thousand-dollar boots."

Tully frowned at her. "It's more tasteful to say 'alligator-skin' boots. The 'three-thousand-dollar' is implied."

"Oh, there I go again, neglecting my boot etiquette."

"Yes! Let this be a lesson to you."

Tully went into his office and called Pap. "Bring your big van and pick me up. We need something big enough for two caskets and ourselves."

"I assume the department will pay me mileage. It doesn't pay me for anything else."

"Yes, it will pay your mileage. I assume the van gets about ten miles per gallon."

"Five. On downhill grades. With a strong wind coming from behind. Do I have to go, too? You finally exhausted me, Bo."

"Yeah, I may need some help. And I can't afford to haul another one of my deputies up there."

"I take it we're headed back to Angst."

"You got it."

Tully was waiting out in front of the courthouse when Pap pulled up in the van.

"I had forgotten just how big this monster is," Tully said, climbing into it. "A rear seat and still enough room for two caskets."

"Probably could squeeze a third coffin in

there, but I'm leaving that space for a nap. You got me plumb wore out, Bo. I used the van for camping back in my youthful sixties. Had a mattress in the back and curtains on the windows. It was nice. What all are we hauling?"

"Just the two caskets. Thought we'd hold a little burial service up at Quail Creek Ranch. I've dealt with a lot of murder victims, but these two strike me as especially sad. You saw how hard Tom and Sean worked, and right when they struck it rich somebody killed them."

He pulled out his cell phone and dialed the ranch. Bernice answered, and he had her put Ernie on.

"Yeah, boss?"

Tully said, "I know how hard you've been working, Thorpe, but here's another chore for you. Have Agatha find a nice last resting place for Tom and Sean on the ranch and you dig two graves there."

"Geez, that's a lot of work! How about I hire some logging types and have them dig the graves? There's a lot of guys out of work around here who would be glad to do it for a few bucks."

"I don't care how you do it, Ernie, just get it done. I want to hold the service today."

"You bringing some cash to pay the loggers? I don't want them to dig the graves and then dump me in one of them."

"I'm bringing Pap."

"Gotcha."

"You can do the driving, Bo," Pap said. "I'm too tired." Tully got out and walked around the van to the driver's side. Pap slid across the seat. Tully drove over to the medical examiner's lab. Susan or one of her helpers had packaged the remains of Tom and Sean in sealed plastic bags. The assistants placed the bags in the coffins and put name tags on the outside.

"You retain all the evidence we might need?" he asked Susan.

"Need for what?" she said. "You don't think there will be a trial after eighty years, do you?"

"Probably not."

"We did take photos of the injuries, which make it clear they were both shot in the back of the head."

"Good. I'll see you when I get back."

"You'd better."

21

Tully turned the van back into Blight City.

"I thought we were headed for Angst," Pap said.

"We are. It just occurred to me that it wouldn't hurt to have a man of the cloth at the burial service. So maybe I can persuade Flynn to come along and officiate."

"A Catholic priest? How do you know the departed were Catholic?"

"I don't. The kid's name was O'Boyle, though. That sounds Irish. I figure Flynn will know some words to cover just about any belief, if any."

Tully walked into the rectory without knocking and found the priest in the kitchen eating breakfast, a tuna-fish sandwich with a glass of milk. The priest frowned up at Tully. "I know this can't be good."

"I need a favor, Flynn," Tully said.

"I knew it," Father James Flynn said.

Tully explained about the murders and

the burial service up on Quail Creek Ranch. He said there was a good chance the O'Boyle boy was Catholic, the name sounding Irish. He didn't know about Agatha's father. He had never known Agatha or Bernice to be religious, but he figured the priest could give the burial service a nice touch.

"Are you turning religious, Bo?" the priest said. "How come? Been having chest pains?"

"None of your business," Tully said. "Are you coming or not?"

The priest chewed the last of his sandwich, finished off his glass of milk, pushed back from the table, and put the dish and silverware in the sink. "It so happens Agatha and Bernice are among my most-favorite people in the entire world, too."

"I hope you're not saying that just because the ranch is the best quail hunting in the state."

"Heaven forbid. The fact is I'm very fond of those two ladies, and if you think it would give them some comfort for me to participate in the ceremony, I will certainly do so."

Half an hour later, the three of them were headed for the little town of Famine, to pick up Dave Perkins at Dave's House of Fry. The gas gauge on the huge van was the first one Tully had ever seen actually move. It touched empty just before they arrived at the town of Famine. Fumes alone took them into the little town. He pulled into Famine's only gas station with its lone pump, the regular. The boy attending the pumps couldn't have been older than twelve.

"I see two coffins in back," he said. "You got bodies in them?"

"Yeah," said Tully. "One of them is a boy not much older than you."

"Gee," the kid said. "That's kind of sad. What happened, Sheriff?"

"They were murdered."

"What you going to do with them?"

Tully studied the boy. He seemed sincere. "We're taking them up to Angst to bury them on a ranch near where the boy lived. We're putting together a little burial service."

The boy pondered this for a moment. "Can I come along? Angst ain't that far."

Tully looked at Pap. The old man shrugged.

"The more the merrier," Tully said.

"I'll go ask my mom. She owns the station now. The old owner is in prison."

"I know," Tully said. "I put him there."

The kid ran into the station and came back with his mother, a stern-looking woman in men's bib overalls and straggly gray-brown hair sticking out from under an old felt hat. She looked in the back of the van at the coffins. "That's real sad," she said. "A youngster scarcely older than Jim here and somebody murdered him. There's some mighty mean folks in the world. Can you get Jim back this evening, Sheriff? I need him around the station."

"I'll get him back," Tully said. "He'll make a good addition to our little group of mourners."

As they pulled out of the station, Flynn said, "We're picking up Dave the Indian, aren't we? He's pretty fond of Agatha and Bernice."

"Sure," Pap said. "He's waiting for us. As a matter of fact he can have my seat. I'm going to lay down in back and catch some shut-eye."

"Don't tell me you're going to lie down between those two coffins," Flynn said.

"Why not? Those fellas won't cause me any mischief."

"You're right about that," Tully said. He motioned with his thumb toward the back. "At least two of them back there won't bother us with their snoring."

He drove over to Dave's House of Fry. Dave was looking for them from a window in his dining room. He came out and climbed into the van's front seat next to the priest.

"Hello, Flynn. Looks as if we're getting together for a hunt."

"I wish we were, Dave."

"It's four months to quail season, Padre," Tully said. "Not that it makes too much difference to a man of the cloth."

The priest laughed. "Just because your Blight Way habits haven't rubbed off on me, don't be suggesting I violate game laws. I am most happy to officiate at an unofficial burial, however, despite its unusual nature and not at all because it involves the owner of the finest quail hunting in the state."

Dave nodded at Jim. "So what brings the boy along?"

"Probably because he leads a life almost as dull as the rest of ours," Tully said. "Right, Jim?"

"I just thought it was sad, burying a kid."

"I like a lad with sensitivity," Dave said. "You don't see that much anymore. I just hope his hanging out with this crowd won't erode it. Speaking of that, where's Pap?"

"He's snoozing back between the coffins," Tully said. "He can sleep just about anywhere. That's Jim back there, Dave, in case you don't know him. He's going to the burial with us."

"Jim pumps my gas all the time," Dave said. "So what's the plan, Bo?"

"Well, the first order of business, we'll get Tom and Sean laid to rest. Then I want to go visit the Finches again. I've brought along a search warrant, just in case they turn out to be fussy about such things."

"A search warrant? What are we searching for?"

"A rolling-block rifle. Remember when Margaret said they had a whole basement full of guns Teddy's grandfather had collected? There may be a rolling-block or two down there."

"You think Teddy's grandfather may have murdered Tom and the boy?" Dave said.

"It's crossed my mind. Suppose Jack Finch happened upon their little mine. He goes inside and sees the veins of gold in the quartz. He kills Tom and Sean before they can file a claim. He blasts the rock cliff up above and buries the mine with the bodies inside. Then he goes up on top and sinks a shaft down until he hits the gold-bearing ore of the little mine. The Finches eventually take millions in gold out of that mine."

"You're saying he shafted the little mine, not to mention Tom and Sean. You think Jack Finch was the kind of man to do that, a man who would kill two people just to make himself incredibly rich?"

Tully turned north on the highway to Angst. "You may remember, Dave, that Teddy said his father would break into a sweat and start to shake at the mere mention of Jack's name. And that was after Jack had been dead for several years! There were some pretty fierce characters running around back in those days. You read some of the articles they wrote for newspapers about their early days and they sound like comical old characters, like every one of them had studied under Mark Twain, but in fact they were hard and mean and willing to do whatever it took to amass a fortune."

Dave said, "Besides the millions in gold the Finches extracted from the mine, you've probably forgotten Pap's take. With its price right now, Pap probably has a thousand dollars' worth of gold in that ketchup bottle."

"I'm sure he's got that figured out," Tully said. "No wonder he was so anxious to find it."

The priest said, "Wait a minute, Bo. I just thought of something. I hope Jim and I aren't going to be stuck up here while you pursue some dangerous criminal."

"Naw, Flynn. I'd never do that to Jim. I've got Deputy Ernie Thorpe up here. I'll send you and Jim back with him in his patrol car.

210

I should point out that patrol car may have been the occasion of sin, if I know Thorpe. You may want to speak to him about that, Padre."

They passed a woman walking along the highway. Dave turned and looked back. "Hold up a second, Bo. That woman looks like she's been beaten up. She's walking barefoot, too."

Tully slowed to a stop and backed up. He pulled over next to the woman, got out of the van, and walked around to where she was plodding along, staring off into the distance. He opened his jacket so she could see his gun and the badge on his belt. She turned and looked at him, then down at the badge.

"I ain't done nothin'," she said.

"I don't know about that, Miss, but somebody has beaten you up. Both your eyes are black and your lip is split and swollen."

"Yeah," she said. "Bud is a mean drunk."

"What's your name?"

"Judy York."

"What's Bud's name?"

"Tanzy. Bud Tanzy."

"How come he beat you up, Judy?"

"No reason. He just got drunk and started waving his gun around. After a while he went to sleep and I split."

"Where are you going, Judy?"

"Don't know. I'm just going."

"I want you to go with us. First I'll take you to a hospital. Then we'll figure out a place for you to stay. You can't just wander along the road."

"Okay," she said.

Tully took her by the hand and began leading her back to the van. "What kind of occupation does Bud have, if any?"

"He robs places."

"He does? Convenience stores by any chance?"

"Yeah, every night he goes out and robs another store. He never gets much money. If I was going to rob something, I'd rob a bank."

"I would, too," Tully said. "Bud must be pretty dumb."

"Dumb and mean."

He opened a door of the van for her. "So where is Bud right now?"

"He's asleep in that old shack of a house down the road a piece. I waited till he was asleep and then took off."

Tully helped her into the backseat of the van and introduced her to the others. "Judy tells me the guy who beat her up is asleep in an old house back down the road a ways. She says he robs convenience stores about

212

every night. He appears to be the guy Daisy told me about. So we're going to turn around and drive back a bit."

"You going to shoot him, Sheriff?" Jim said, suddenly interested.

"I'd like to, but I think I'll just arrest him. Dave, open the glove compartment and see if there's a piece of rope in there."

Dave opened the compartment. "Nope. A ball of some fairly heavy twine, though."

"That will do."

Tully turned the truck around and headed back down the road.

"There's the house," Judy said.

Tully turned the van around and parked it on the edge of the highway. He got out and walked down the driveway to the house. The place looked as if it were about to fall down. He stepped very quietly onto the rickety porch and stopped to listen. Faint sounds of snoring came from inside. He drew his gun, turned the knob on the door, opened it slightly, and peeked in. A man was asleep on an old couch. A half-empty bottle of whiskey sat on the chair next to the couch. A revolver was next to the bottle. The man wore only pants and an undershirt. Tully tiptoed up next to him and placed the muzzle of his 9 mm Colt Commander against his temple. The man's eyes popped open.

"Relax, partner. You're under arrest for assault and battery and armed robbery."

The man heaved what Tully interpreted to be a sigh of relief. "Scared me," he said. "I thought it was Judy. There really ain't no reason to arrest me."

"You rob stores," Tully said. "You're the 'Eight O'clock Robber.'"

The man took a moment to reply. "Well, yeah, I guess."

Tully had Tanzy put on his shirt and shoes and a rumpled suit jacket he found in a closet. Then tied his hands behind him with the twine.

"Hey, that's too tight," Tanzy said. "It's cutting into my wrists."

"What's your point?" Tully said. "I'm not sure this twine will hold you, Bud, but you better hope it does. I have a serious dislike of men who beat up women." He picked up Tanzy's gun and slipped it into a pocket of his jacket.

He put Tanzy in the backseat of the van with the boy and Judy. "Don't worry, Judy, his hands are tied. There's a tire iron on the floor back there. If he tries anything, hit him across the nose with it. That will get his attention."

Judy called Tanzy an obscene name.

"Watch the language," Tully said. "We have a priest here. Also Jim."

Judy turned to Jim. "Sorry, kid."

"That's okay. I hear it in school all the time."

"Yeah," Tully said. "Those teachers get tougher all the time."

"I should have gone to school," Tanzy said. He turned and looked into the rear section of the van. "What are those coffins doing back here?"

Tully explained about the coffins.

"Too bad," Tanzy said. "At least I never killed nobody."

"That makes three people in this van who haven't," Tully said. "So you might want to be on your best behavior, Bud."

Dave said, "What are we going to do if we run into Lucas now?"

"Then it's every man for himself. Woman, too."

"You talking about Lucas Kincaid?" Judy said.

"Shut up, Judy!" Tanzy shouted and shoved against her. She reached down on the floor and picked up the tire iron. Tanzy shrank back.

"That's exactly who we're talking about," Dave said. "Why, you know him?"

Judy tapped the tire iron up and down on the palm of her hand. "He stayed overnight at our place a couple days ago!"

"Shut up, Judy! You don't know nothing."

"I know something! He took all our food and money!"

"Shut up, I told you! He'll come back and kill us both! We're lucky to get out alive as it is!"

Tully tipped up the brim of his Stetson, and glanced back at Tanzy. "Took all your money, did he? How much did he get?"

Tanzy shrugged. "Fifty-two dollars and change. When Lucas asks you for something, you best give it to him. You give it all to him."

"How come you know Kincaid, anyway?"

"Met him in prison a year ago. He was one angry old man. Said he felt like killing half the county, but you were first on his list, Sheriff."

"He's already killed four people since he got out, so I guess I've moved down the list."

Judy moaned. "He'll kill us all he gets the chance! You got any idea where he is now, Sheriff?"

Tully tugged the droopy corner of his mustache. "No, I don't. I wish I did but I don't. I think he intends to hide out in the Snowies. If he does that, we may never find him. What puzzles me is why he wants money. There's no place to spend money in the mountains."

"He's probably putting together a grub-stake," Pap said. "Fifty-two dollars will buy a lot of dried beans."

Judy poked Tanzy in the belly with the end of the tire iron. "If Lucas goes into a store to buy anything, they'll probably give him whatever he wants just to get rid of him. He stinks to high heaven."

"Yeah," Tanzy agreed. "He stunk bad in prison, too. When the guards couldn't stand it anymore, I think they hosed him down. Probably from a distance, because he can snap your neck like a twig."

"I don't recall he smelled all that bad when I arrested him," Tully said. "Maybe it was a hobby he took up later. By the way, Bud, how come you went back to robbing stores as soon as you got out of prison?"

"It was the only work I knew."

"Sounds reasonable."

22

They arrived in Angst with enough gas to get them to the service station. "Fill her up," Tully told the attendant.

"What are those coffins doing back there?" the attendant asked.

Tully explained once again about the remains. The man shook his head and began filling the tank.

Pap suddenly sat up between the caskets. "What's going on?" he said.

Tully leaned out his window and yelled. "Stop that! You're spraying gas all over. It's only my father!"

The attendant was wild-eyed. "I don't care who it is! Get it out of here!"

Tully finally got the man calmed down. Pap began to climb over into the backseat.

"Stay away from me!" yelled Tanzy.

"You guys are starting to hurt my feelings," Pap said, sliding into the rear seat next to Judy. "I don't know how an old man is expected to get any sleep with all the blabbing going on."

Tully told them Pap had only been resting.

"I was plumb wore out," Pap said. "I guess I did sleep like I was dead."

"My nerves can't take much more of this," Tanzy said.

Tully handed Tanzy's revolver to Pap and told him to use it if Tanzy tried to escape.

"I got my own," Pap said.

"I know you do. But if you use it we'll probably have to throw it away. So take Tanzy's. We can't be throwing away expensive guns!"

"Good thinking," Pap said. He took the revolver.

"If you think you're scaring me," Tanzy said, "you are. I've never been arrested by cops this crazy!"

"Thanks," Pap said.

After dropping Pap and the others off at Jake's Café for lunch, Tully intended to take Judy to the local emergency room, but she said there was nothing wrong with her that a little makeup wouldn't cure. So he rented a motel room and sent Judy into the bathroom to take a shower. Then he went to JCPenney and bought her a dress, two blouses, a pair of slacks, nylons, underwear, white socks, white sneakers, and makeup. He put it all on the county credit card. He returned in less than an hour. Judy, a pink towel wrapped around her, was seated on the bed. She took the cartons and bags into the bathroom. When she came out dressed in some of her new clothes, lipsticked, powdered, rouged, and eye-shadowed, she looked almost pretty. With a hairdo, she would have been.

"I can't believe you did all this for me," she said. "I can't believe anyone would, let alone a cop."

"I'm not finished," Tully said. "Blight County may be a little backward compared with other parts of the country, but it looks after its own. And you're part of its own."

Tully went down to the motel office to check out. "We should get a cut rate," he told the clerk at the counter. "We were here only about an hour."

"Most of our clients usually are," the clerk said. "Fifteen dollars."

Tully decided it was best to pay in cash. He and Judy walked over to Jake's Café. Pap had untied Tanzy's hands so he could eat. They had finished their lunch and were chatting like a bunch of old friends. Judy said some of her teeth were sore and ordered only the soup. Tully ordered a hamburger.

No one apparently had ordered the Canadian hash.

After Tully had tied up Tanzy's hands again, they climbed back into the van and headed for Quail Creek Ranch. "So, who's officiating at this burial?" Flynn asked.

"I figured you would," Tully said. "You're probably the only one here who knows the words."

"We don't even know if the boy was Catholic," the priest said. "Certainly Agatha has never mentioned religion to me. You know what she is, Bo?"

"Basically, an ornery old lady," Tully said. "She was a fierce teacher, I can tell you that. You learned your Shakespeare whether you wanted to or not. She single-handedly turned me from Pap's son into a civilized human being."

"That seems a bit extreme," Flynn said.

"Pap's son?"

"Civilized human being. Have you ever caught him being civilized, Pap?"

"I did once," Pap said, "and it scared me. He could never last as sheriff of Blight County if he was civilized."

"He's been nice to me," Judy said.

"That's because you're a woman," Flynn said. "Bo loves all women."

"My one weakness," Tully said.

"Don't you think that's the perfect formula for sin, Padre?" Dave said.

"I have a hard time keeping up on human chemistry," the priest said.

"I went to church once," Tanzy said.

Pap said, "I guess it didn't take, huh, Tanzy?"

"I kind of liked it. Seemed peaceful or something. My grandmother took me. Then she died and I never went again."

"That's why I don't go," Pap said. "You get that close to God he might decide to snap you up."

The priest shook his head.

They turned off the highway onto the road leading to Quail Creek Ranch. The van thumped and rattled over the rough road. Pap said, "I got an idea what could fix this road for Agatha and Bernice."

"What's that?" Tully said.

"That's for me to know."

Tully stopped in front of the gate.

"My gosh, look at the birds," Judy said. "They look like real birds flying up across the bars."

"Yeah, they do," said Tully. "Pap, get out and open the gate."

"Why is it always me? What's wrong with Flynn or Dave opening it?"

"Because Flynn is a priest and Dave's an

Indian. You don't expect a priest or an Indian to open a gate, do you?"

"That's right," Dave said. "We Indians have a firm principle against opening gates."

Muttering a string of obscenities, Pap got out and opened the gate.

"I should make him walk the rest of the way to the house," Tully said.

"You know he's always armed," Dave said.

"True. So I guess I'll wait for him."

Agatha, Bernice, and Bunny came out to greet them. Ernie Thorpe stood in the doorway of the house, as if guarding it. You can't fool me, you little poacher, Tully thought. "Ernie," he yelled. "You got your cuffs on you?"

"Yeah."

"Well bring them over here and put them on this sorry individual."

Ernie walked out and spun Tanzy around. He pulled out his pocketknife and cut the twine off his hands and started to put on the cuffs.

"Wait," Tully said. "Don't put them on. Tanzy's going to the burial with us. It will be better without the cuffs. If he runs, shoot him and we'll bury him, too."

Tanzy said, "I ain't going to run."

Tully turned to Agatha. "The graves ready?"

"Yes, Bernice and I selected a shady spot on a knoll overlooking the creek and Ernie hired four nice young men from town to dig the graves. They said they could use the work, but when we told them what happened, they said they wouldn't take the money and would stay for the burial. Would it be all right, Bo, if I looked in my father's casket?"

"Not a good idea," he said.

"I suppose after all these years it's just as well. And I still have the pictures."

"Yes, you do."

A white Suburban pulled up behind the van. Susan got out. She said to Agatha, "I got to thinking about the burial service and decided to drive up. I hope that's okay." She was wearing her lab uniform and had obviously rushed up to the ranch from work. Her dark brown hair had been tied in kind of a knot and was starting to come loose. Tully thought she was even more beautiful than usual.

"Oh, that is so thoughtful of you, Susan," Agatha said. "And it's wonderful to see you again. I do hope you're getting back together with Bo."

"We're working on it," she said. "I've given him the ten steps for improvement. We'll have to see how he does on them. This is such a sad occasion, Agatha. I hope you don't mind that I came along uninvited. I brought along some flowers. They're just lilacs, but I had a ton of them growing at the house. I know you've read Whitman's poem about the death of Lincoln."

" 'When Lilacs Last in the Dooryard Bloomed,' " Agatha said. "Lilacs are perfect. I'll have Ernie carry them up to the knoll." That's when she noticed Tanzy. "Good heavens! Who is this?"

"Just another one of my criminals," Tully said. "We picked him up on our way here. And this young lady is Judy. She's going to work for Dave at his House of Fry."

Dave said, "What? Oh, right, I must have forgotten."

"I'm so glad all of you could come," Agatha said. "It would have been such a sad occasion if Bernice and Bunny and I had been the only ones. And Ernie, of course. He's such a nice young man, and he and Bunny get along wonderfully."

Tully glared over Agatha's head at Ernie, who gave one of his innocent shrugs.

As they trudged up to the knoll overlooking Quail Creek, they came to the four grave diggers sitting under a tree smoking cigarettes. Dave stopped in midstride, "Stubb and Gordy!"

"Oh, you've met before!" exclaimed Agatha. The two loggers were as surprised as Dave. Agatha introduced the other two diggers, who had leaped up and were dusting off their jeans.

Father James Flynn gave a brief but fitting talk. Then he asked if anyone there could sing. Jim raised his grease-blackened hand. "Hit it, Jim," Tully said. The kid's voice was high and clear and beautiful and wafted up into the birch branches and drifted out over Quail Creek like some wild thing released from a cage.

Tully had to tug hard on the corner of his mustache to keep tears from welling up. He didn't recognize the hymn and wasn't even sure it was a hymn. Maybe Jim had just made it up. "I was trying to remember why we had brought you along, Jim," he told the boy afterward, "and I guess this was it."

"I'm glad I could do something," Jim said.

They left Stubb and Gordy and the two other loggers to fill in the graves and walked back down to the house.

"You want me to head back to town, boss?" Ernie asked, coming up alongside of Tully.

"Yeah, your little vacation is over. Pap and Dave are staying with me. You take everybody else back into town in your patrol car.

Get Judy a cabin at the Pine Creek Motel."

"As I recall, the owner still hates you."

"Yeah, well tell Janet this is official business and the county will pay the bill. Judy's a witness in the string of robberies. Arrange for her to eat her meals over at Granny's Café."

"That's kind of mean."

"Sure, but it will be a while before she notices. You know what to do with Tanzy. Drop Jim off in Famine and thank his mother for letting him go. Tell him we'll get him an official Blight County sheriff's T-shirt. Tomorrow, bring Lurch up here to pick up the Humvee and check it out."

"What about Kincaid?"

"As soon as I know something, Ernie, I'll tell you."

"Okay if I take Bunny back with us?"

"Yes, take her, you miserable little poacher."

"Thanks, Bo. I'm sorry if I —"

"Never apologize for stealing another man's woman, Ernie, because it won't do you any good. Besides, Susan and I may be back together again, as soon as I improve somewhat. So I guess I'll let you live."

23

Tully pulled the van into the Finch driveway. He, Pap, and Dave got out, walked up to the porch. Dave rang the doorbell. Margaret answered. "My goodness, Sheriff, you're back. Dave and Pap, too. Good to see all of you. Come in, come in!"

"I'm really sorry to bother you, Margaret, but we're back on business, I'm afraid. The last time we were here you happened to mention that your basement was full of firearms."

Teddy Finch walked in at that moment. "So you're back on business I heard you say, Bo. I hope Margaret hasn't been up to something illegal."

Tully laughed. "Not that I know of, Teddy. I'll bring you up to date on the mystery we're trying to solve. I understand you know Agatha Wrenn."

"We do indeed. Both Agatha and Bernice. They're lovely women. Bernice is a wonder-

228

ful artist and Agatha is a distinguished Elizabethan scholar. You think our mine might have something to do with the disappearance of Agatha's father?"

"It's possible. We found a small mine in the drainage directly below the Finch Mine. The cliff above it had been blasted to create a rock slide that covered up the old mine entrance."

Margaret looked shocked. "Good heavens!"

Teddy nodded his head. "You know, Bo, my father knew some secret he said he would tell me someday, but he never did. I think it was something he knew about my grandfather."

"We found the remains of two people in the little mine," Tully said.

Teddy's mouth gaped. Margaret shook her head and appeared about to cry.

"Now for the bad part," Tully said. "Both of them had been murdered. One of them was Agatha's father, the other, Sean O'Boyle, a kid of about fourteen."

"Murdered!" gasped Margaret. "Oh no!"

"I knew my dad's secret must have been something terrible," Teddy said. "That's why he could never bring himself to tell me. What you're thinking, Bo, is that my grandfather discovered that little mine below where the Finch Mine now sits. He killed Agatha's father and the boy, and then filed his own claim and blasted a shaft down from the top of the mountain to intersect the ore."

Margaret looked as if she was about to faint. Dave put his arm around her and eased her into a chair. Teddy sat down on the couch, shaking his head.

"You're right, Teddy, that's what I've been thinking," Tully said. "I hope it doesn't turn out to be the case. What we do know is that each of the victims was killed with a .43-caliber bullet that has a ridge at its base. It was probably fired from a rolling-block rifle used by the Cubans in the Spanish-American War. A lot of American veterans of that war brought the rifles home. You told me that your grandfather was a veteran of the war. It's possible he brought one or two of those rifles back with him. The last time we were here Margaret mentioned you had a basement full of old firearms. So I was hoping you would let us look through them and see if we can find any rolling-blocks."

Teddy seemed dazed. "Of course, Bo, you're welcome to look for whatever you like. I know enough about you to know that you have a warrant on you somewhere, but you don't have to bother with that. If you find something, I'll sign whatever you need to make it official."

Margaret seemed to recover faster than Teddy. She said, "Follow me, Bo. I'll show you the way down to the basement. It's kind of a mess, with guns and boxes of bullets piled everywhere. Teddy has always been going to get everything organized, but he's never got around to it."

Tully had never seen anything like it. Half the basement had been partitioned off into a large room. Racks of rifles covered every wall, and crates were filled with handguns and boxes of bullets.

Tully said, "We're looking for rifles, Margaret, so we shouldn't have to mess with the crates."

"Do whatever you need to, Bo! Just call Teddy or me if you need any help."

"Thanks, Margaret. We'll try to get this done in a hurry so we don't ruin the rest of your evening." He knew he had already ruined something a great deal longer than an evening.

The search went much faster than any of them had expected, given the number of firearms present. Within in an hour they had checked all the racks and found two Remington rolling-block rifles in .43 caliber. Teddy came down to the basement and helped them find a box of cartridges for it. The bullets had turned green. "In Cuba, our troops thought green bullets were poisonous and maybe they were," he said. "They probably had microbes all over them in that hot, moist climate. Many wounded died from infection."

Tully said, "I'll have Lurch fire a round from each of these rifles and compare the striations with the striations on the bullets that killed Tom and the boy. That should tell us if Jack Finch was the fellow who shot them."

"I hate to think our good fortune may have resulted from the murder of two people, but from what I've heard about my grandfather, I wouldn't put it past him."

"It's certainly not your fault, Teddy. I'll give you a call in a couple of days and let you know if the fatal bullets came from either of these two guns."

"However it turns out, I'd appreciate hearing," Teddy said. "I've also got filing boxes of papers from the mine that I've never looked at. They're pretty boring, but I'll check out some of those from the early days and maybe I'll learn something."

"That could be a big help, Teddy. Obviously, whoever committed the murders is long dead and there never will be a trial of any kind, but I told Agatha I would solve the mystery for her if I could. So that's what I'm doing."

"I understand completely, Bo. I want to know, too. Also, I'd like to do something for Agatha."

"If you're thinking about giving her money, she would never accept it," Tully said.

Pap looked up from a crate of handguns he'd been inspecting. "I'll tell you something she might appreciate. You could give her that big pile of slag you got up at the mine. It must have been setting there for a hundred years."

"What on earth would she do with that?" Tully said.

"For one thing, she's got that road that needs surfacing. I think the slag would make a heck of a road."

"That's a wonderful idea, Pap!" Teddy said. "I'll write you out a paper giving her ownership of the whole pile."

"Great! I'll have a couple of dump trucks and a loader come in and pick it up tomorrow."

"You sure it's something she'll like, Pap?" Teddy asked.

"She'll love it, Teddy, she'll love it!"

24

"Not the gun," Lurch said. "I've tested them both and neither is the gun that killed the guys in the mine."

"You're sure, Lurch?"

"Positive."

"I can't say I'm sorry," Tully said, propping his alligator-skin boots up on his desk. "I don't think this clears Jack Finch, though. Margaret and Teddy aren't going to be satisfied. Jack could have used another .43-caliber gun and ditched it somewhere. On the other hand, when your son is named after Theodore Roosevelt and your grandson is, too, I kind of doubt you would ditch a weapon you had picked up during your campaign in Cuba with Roosevelt's Rough Riders. It's one heck of a souvenir. I think the rifles you just checked are only some of the rifles Jack brought home with him. There's a third .43-caliber rifle somewhere. Or at least there was."

"I'm sorry it wasn't one of these, boss."

"Yeah, I'm sorry, too. It would have wrapped this mystery up for Agatha. At least she's getting a nice road out of it."

"How come?"

"Pap is up at the Finch Mine right now, loading a huge pile of slag onto dump trucks. I guess the slag will crunch up into a nice surface."

"You trust Pap a whole lot more than you used to."

"Nope, Lurch, I don't. He's got me worried sick about the whole deal."

Lurch went back to his computer shaking his head.

Tully dialed Susan. "How about lunch, sweetheart?"

"Anytime, Bo," her assistant said. "But we'd better not let Susan find out."

"Good idea, Amy," he said.

Susan came on laughing. He knew Amy had told her. He had forgotten they sounded almost identical on the phone. Amy isn't that bad looking, either, he thought. "Ah," he said, "at last I've got the right sweetheart."

"Yes, you do. Lunch sounds great."

"Super," he said. "I'll meet you at Crabbs."

"Why do we always eat at Crabbs?"

"Because I don't have to think what to order for lunch at Crabbs. I always get the beef dip and fries, and it's always good."

"That's what I like about you, Bo, your sense of adventure."

"Usually I don't go to such extremes. See you at noon." He hung up.

Daisy yelled at him through the open door. "Pick up on two, Bo. It's a Mr. Finch."

Bo shuddered. Pap had probably been caught up to no good. "Hello, Teddy," he said. "It's about Pap, isn't it?"

"Pap? No, I haven't seen Pap. You worried something happened to him, Bo?"

"No, Teddy, not at all. What can I do for you?"

"You know how I told you I was going to look through those old papers we took out of the mine office?"

"Yeah."

"Well, I found something of interest. My grandfather didn't start the mine. A man by the name of Blunt did, Howard Blunt. He took Jack Finch on as a partner about a year after the mine started. Six months later there is no mention of Blunt. From then on, the mine is called Finch."

"What happened to Blunt?"

"I don't know. He just vanished. Maybe they had a falling-out. I suspect Jack Finch was the kind of man you didn't want to have a falling-out with. I looked through dozens of papers and there is just no mention of Blunt. There's some indication this Blunt fellow and my grandfather joined the Rough Riders together."

"I think I see where you're going with this, Teddy. If Jack Finch signed onto the mine after it got started, he probably wasn't the one who discovered Tom's little mine. Therefore, he wasn't the one who killed Tom and the boy."

"That's where I'm going with it, Bo."

"You got any idea what happened to Howard Blunt?"

"Just my guess."

"About the same as mine, I bet. You know of any Blunts live around here, Teddy?"

"No, not around here. There's a Blunt that owns an accounting firm in Spokane. It's an unusual name. He could be a descendent."

"It so happens I have to make a trip to Spokane. I'll check him out."

At lunch, Tully went with beef dip and fries and Susan went with the fish-and-chips. "I have to admit," she said, "Crabbs has the best fish-and-chips in all of Idaho. England, on the other hand, has the best fish-and-chips in the world."

"You've been to England?"

"Yes, when I was twelve. My father and mother took us four girls with them when Dad was on a sabbatical from the university. We lived in an apartment down in Cornwall for a month. The fish-and-chips were absolutely scrumptious!"

"I've never been anywhere," Tully said. "I'd like to get to England someday. Maybe we could go together."

"Maybe," she said. "You would have to be a lot more attentive, though."

"I'm working on it," he said. He wondered if the flyboy had been attentive. Apparently not.

"I do think you're still hung up on your wife, Bo. It's been ten years since Ginger died. It's really time you put that part of your life behind you. People have to move on."

"I have moved on," he said.

"But not all that far."

25

He pulled his sheriff's department Explorer up in front of Jean Runyan's art gallery in Spokane, took the painting out of the back, and hauled it inside. Jean was an attractive woman with gray, neatly coifed hair and deceptively kind eyes behind rimless glasses. "Oh, Bo, wonderful to see you! I've been hoping you would bring me something. But it's huge."

He stood the painting up and turned it around so she could see it.

"Oh, my gosh!" she said. "It's wonderful! I have patrons of who will kill for that painting!"

"Here's the thing," he said. "I want Sid Brown to have first shot at it."

"But, Bo, you're depriving me of a bloodbath among Spokane's art patrons!"

"I'm sorry, but I want Sid to have it."

"He'll have to offer at least twenty grand."

"I expect he will. I don't have his phone

number, Jean, but he owns the Giggling Loon restaurant in Boise."

"I know Sid," she said. "I've sold him half a dozen of your watercolors at ridiculously low prices. Now he's going to pay!"

Tully turned and left, so he wouldn't have to hear Jean's merciless laugh. It was the sort of thing that could haunt a person's dreams.

Raymond Blunt's office was on the top floor of the Blunt Building, an indication that the Blunt family had done all right for itself over the years. He told the receptionist he was Sheriff Bo Tully to see Mr. Blunt.

The girl turned pale and gasped, "Not again!"

Tully imagined her boss scurrying down a rear fire escape. "I'm not here on enforcement business," he told her. "I just need some information about his grandfather."

The girl disappeared through a door behind her and presently returned with a bald, wizened little man not over five-foot-five. His white eyebrows were bunched up in a frown.

"What is it you want?" he growled.

"I would like some information about your grandfather," Tully said, "if Howard Blunt was your grandfather."

The little man responded with a facial tic,

then said, "Come on back to my office."

The office was large and old with a great deal of dark wood on the walls and four tiny windows on two sides of the corner office. Blunt motioned to a chair in front of his desk. Tully sat down.

"So what is it you want to know about my grandfather?" he asked.

Tully thought he should give Blunt a little background first. He explained about the murders of Tom Link and Sean O'Boyle.

"Sounds like something my grandfather might have been involved in," Blunt said. "My understanding is that he was a thoroughly nasty man. My own father, who wasn't exactly a prince of a human being, was terrified of him."

"Must have been the standard for fathers in those days," Tully said. "Do you know if your grandfather was a member of Teddy Roosevelt's Rough Riders?"

"Yes, I certainly do. I tired of hearing about it at a very young age."

"Apparently, he and Jack Finch joined up together and were buddies all through the Spanish-American War. From what I have been able to learn, your grandfather started what became known as the Finch Mine."

"That's my understanding. Then one day he simply disappeared without leaving a trace. From what I understand, my family at the time was not in the least grieved to have him vanish. They generally felt they owed Jack Finch a debt of gratitude."

"So they thought Finch had something to do with your grandfather's disappearance?"

"Oh, yes. If you'd known Jack Finch, I think you might have, too. He apparently was an unholy terror."

Tully tugged thoughtfully on the corner of his mustache.

"The reason I'm here, Mr. Blunt, is that I'm looking for the weapon used in the murder of a miner named Tom Link and a fourteen-year-old boy by the name of Sean O'Boyle. I suspect your grandfather may have brought back a .43-caliber rolling-block rifle with him from Cuba. The bullets for it probably would have been green, not unusual, but the moist climate of Cuba may have made them even greener."

Blunt leaned back in his chair and rolled his eyes up toward the ceiling. After a bit he said, "I'm not much of a gun person, Sheriff, but I do remember a box of green bullets. I gave both the bullets and the rifle to one of our local museums. The curators were putting together a display of Spanish-American War artifacts involving people from this area. Apparently, the war was quite popular with our residents at the time. I'm not much of a museum person, so I don't know if the display ever got set up or not."

Tully thanked Blunt and told him if he ever determined the rifle at the museum was the murder weapon, he would let him know.

"Don't bother," Blunt growled.

26

The museum was a large boxy affair with a great deal of exterior metal and glass. Tully wasn't much of a museum person, either, and the place made him nervous. Museums always gave him the feeling he was supposed to know something he had never even heard of. A striking young woman took him back to the director's office, her high heels clicking smartly on the floor, reminding him of Daisy. She knocked on a door and was told to enter. The room turned out to be a workshop of some sort and the director was dressed in a pair of dusty gray coveralls. The young woman said, "Sheriff Tully, this is our director, Mr. Mullan," and then left. Tully could hear her footsteps receding down the museum hallway.

"Sheriff Bo Tully," the director said. "I am aware of your reputation, as an artist that is. I'm afraid I don't follow the crime scene much."

"That's fine with me," Tully said. "But it's the crime scene that brings me here."

"Indeed? Well, how may I be of service to you in that regard?"

Tully told him about the 1927 murders of Tom Link and Sean O'Boyle and the rifle that may have been used in the killings.

The director said, "Nineteen twenty-seven! You take your crime-solving very seriously, Sheriff."

"Yes, I do. Usually, I don't take on crimes quite this old, but one of the victims was the father of a friend of mine. I suspect there may have been a third murder, but I will be satisfied if I can simply find the rifle that was used in the first two. I assume you keep a record of the various donors. The rifle I'm looking for was donated to the museum by a Mr. Raymond Blunt."

"Ray Blunt. Yes, I know him well. Quite the jovial individual."

"That was my impression."

The director laughed. "I believe we have three Cuban rifles in the exhibit, but the one from Ray Blunt will be identified as such. Come with me and we'll go take a look."

The exhibit showed three mannequins dressed in Cuban uniforms, each holding a rifle. They were surrounded by Rough Riders, one of whom bore a slight resemblance to Theodore Roosevelt. There was an open box of the green bullets at the feet of one of the Cubans.

"The Cuban soldier on the far right is the one holding the rifle donated by Ray Blunt," the director said, referring to a note on the edge of the exhibit.

"Excellent, Mr. Mullan. Now I'm afraid I must take that rifle with me to have it checked by my CSI unit."

"Oh, I'm afraid I can't permit that," said Mr. Mullan.

Tully gave him The Look.

"Oh, you're right of course, Sheriff. I'll have to have you sign some papers, though."

"No problem."

Tully spent the night at the Davenport Hotel in Spokane and drove back to Blight City in the morning, stopping first at the office. The law-enforcement business seemed to be humming smoothly along under Daisy's firm command, even though he knew his undersheriff would take credit for it.

"Looks like you've got everything under control, Herb," he said, giving Daisy a wink. She rolled her eyes.

Herb said, "Yeah, but I'm glad you're back, Bo. This job is wearing me to a frazzle." He went back to reading his paper. Tully had noticed that in any institution or business, there are always individuals who do absolutely nothing. This was Herb's function.

As usual, Lurch was hunched over his computer. He probably had already solved three crimes that morning.

"I've got a job for you, Lurch," Tully said. "Something a little more interesting than your usual fare. It's the rifle that may have been used in the mine murders. Check out the striations on its bullets against those we found in the mine."

Lurch beamed at him. "Great!"

"The gun's in the back of my Explorer. I guess you can use your water tank to fire the gun into."

"Right. As soon as I have the bullet, I'll head down to the crime lab in Pocatello to make the comparison."

"I guess that will take you through Boise," Tully said. "Why don't you spend the night there on the way back? Take Sarah out to dinner at the Giggling Loon restaurant. Put it on your county charge card."

Lurch stopped and stared at his boss as if he thought the sheriff had gone mad. "I'll do it!" he said, grinning. "Sarah would love that!"

Sarah was the gorgeous and brilliant medical scientist in a Boise hospital. Why she took to Lurch, Tully couldn't fathom. He suspected failing eyesight on her part, all that time spent looking through microscopes. Although he was fond of Lurch himself, he couldn't imagine what kind of girl would fall in love with his CSI unit. Oh, yeah, Sarah was a scientist and Lurch was brilliant. He probably was attentive, too.

"What are you thinking?" the unit said, stopping on his way out.

"Nothing, Lurch. Get going before I do think of something."

He walked into his office. Daisy followed him in. "So what hideous messes have occurred while I've been gone?" he asked her.

"Just the routine," she said.

"That bad, huh?"

"Yeah, it never ends." She sat down in a chair across from him. As always, she was a model of perfect efficiency, her back ramrod straight, her legs crossed beneath her black skirt, the white blouse perfect.

Daisy is something else, he thought. Now that she's divorced, she's also available. So many women, so little time. "So how is our jail population getting along?"

"Oh, they're grousing as usual. A couple of them tried to climb out of the playpen

248

the other day. Herb put down his newspaper long enough to fire a shotgun in the air. Scared the wits out of them. Ever since then they've occupied themselves with basketball."

"Who were the two miscreants?"

"Oh, Vince and Otto. They share almost a whole brain. Maybe you should think about getting some tax to expand the jail, especially the playpen."

"If I ever get the urge to raise taxes, it will be to improve the wages around here. I don't think we have one deputy with a decent car of his own. Pugh is still driving that ratty old blue Ford pickup he's had for about thirty years."

"Brian loves that pickup, Bo."

"I know. All us old Idaho boys love our pickups. Speaking of Brian, I don't suppose you've heard anything from him."

"No, nothing."

"I'm starting to think we never will."

"Don't say that, Bo!"

"Sorry," he said. "Anyway, it would be nice to get a new pickup once in a while. Come to think of it, I've never had a new pickup. By 'new,' of course, I mean one not more than ten years old."

Daisy said, "A raise would be wonderful, Bo! Can we count on that?"

Tully laughed. "No! The strain of my being gone must have affected your sanity. You know how folks around here feel about taxes. Of much greater importance is that the mention of taxes would certainly have an adverse effect on my next election. We don't want to do anything that might threaten that, do we?"

"Oh, you know your Freezer Day guarantees your next election."

He noticed the cartoon he had drawn of Susan on his desk calendar. He ripped off the page, wadded it up, and threw it in the wastebasket. "You think? Well, I suppose I should wander down to the jail and check on our criminals."

"You should, Bo. You know they're always so happy to see you."

"Right." He headed down to the basement.

Lulu, the jail matron, opened the door for him. "Hi, Bo."

"Hi, Lulu. How's it going?"

"Not bad, but don't go over to the women's side. They're having a hissy fit of some kind. As soon as I'm done with my tea, I'll go shut them up."

"I'll take a look at the men. Anyone of interest in there?"

"Naw. Just the regulars and your stick-up

man, Tanzy."

He opened the door to the men's section and walked in. Someone called out, "Snap to, everybody. It's Bo, come for a visit!"

Instantly there arose a great yammering of voices and pounding on bars with various objects. He walked along the cells, looking in. He knew all the inmates. Lulu was right, all the regulars. Suddenly he stopped, backed up, and took a second look into a cell. "Petey! What are you doing back in here?"

"It's all a big mistake, Bo!" the little man cried. "I was walking home from your Freezer Day and saw this chain saw on the sidewalk. It looked just like mine. I figured somebody must of stole it, so I picked it up and took it home."

"Petey, you're not a chain saw kind of guy and you know it. You fall down on one of those things, they bury you in a dozen quart jars."

"I hate it in here!" Petey yelled, very much the enraged pixie. "These guys are a mean bunch!"

Tully had to smile. "That's one of the downsides of being a criminal, Petey — the company you get to keep!"

He walked to the end of the row of cells. "Guess what, fellows," he shouted. "I've ordered in sirloin steak, baked potatoes, and salad with blue cheese dressing for each of you tonight. Crabbs is preparing it all right now."

Cheers went up from the cells.

Tully laughed. "You guys are so easy. I was joking! Can you imagine what the commissioners would do if they caught me feeding my criminals a bunch of steak dinners from Crabbs with all the fixings?" He slammed the door behind him to shut off the screamed obscenities. People stupid enough to end up in jail just don't have the intelligence to appreciate a good joke.

He returned to the briefing room, tugging thoughtfully on his mustache.

"Daisy, how many jokers we got locked up down there?"

"Six women and ten men. Why?"

"Call up Crabbs and order sixteen steak dinners with all the fixings. Have them delivered tonight."

"Have you gone crazy, Bo! The commissioners will howl like banshees."

"They howl no matter what. Give them something to howl about, I always say."

27

The next morning Tully had barely fizzed out his usual half cup of coffee when Lurch called. "We got a match, boss!"

"Great!"

He went into his office and dialed Agatha's number. Bernice answered.

"Hi, Bernice. It's Bo. Pap was going to help you out with that road into the ranch. I was wondering if he got around to it."

"Oh, my goodness, yes! Agatha is going to have the whole thing paved."

"Paved?"

"Yes. And there will be money left over."

"Money?"

"Yes, Pap called yesterday and said the smelter up in Trail called yesterday and said there were forty-three ounces of gold in the slag. They said at today's gold prices that amounts to thirty-eight thousand seven hundred dollars."

Tully frowned. "Pap set this up?"

"Yes, without even telling us. Agatha was in total shock. She called the Finches right away and said she couldn't take the money, but Teddy said she had to take it, because all he had given her was an old pile of slag. So she finally gave in. She's been calling contractors all morning to find out how much it would cost to get the road paved."

"Pap set this up?" Tully repeated, still frowning.

"Yes, he really is a dear man. Not many men would go to all this trouble for two old ladies. I'm actually sorry I've called him such rather harsh names from time to time."

Tully was now frowning and shaking his head. "So Pap set this up? Is Agatha handy?"

"Hold on a second, Bo, I'll get her."

Agatha came on. "Oh, Bo, it's so good to hear from you. I guess Bernice has already told you the wonderful thing Pap has done. I tried to give the money back to the Finches, but they refused. They said the pile of slag had sat there for eighty years or more and as far as they were concerned it was totally worthless. They insisted I keep the money, so I am."

"And Pap set this up?"

"Yes, and now I have to take back all the nasty things I've said about him over the years, at least those I can remember."

I would be glad to help your memory, Tully thought, but I won't. He said, "Agatha, I have some news about the death of your dad and Sean O'Boyle."

He heard her suck in her breath. "What, Bo?"

"We found the gun that was used."

"Oh, dear! And it belonged to Jack Finch."

"I am happy to tell you that it didn't. It belonged to a man named Howard Blunt, who became a partner of Jack Finch a year or two after Blunt had started the mine that Jack Finch later named the Finch Mine. Oddly, Blunt disappeared without a trace shortly before Jack took over the mine. But since Blunt was the one who started the mine, it is very likely he was the one who discovered Tom and Sean's mine down on the side of the mountain. We can tie the murder weapon to him, although we can't say definitely who pulled the trigger. My guess is that it was Blunt himself."

He waited. There was no sound at the other end of the line.

"Agatha?"

The old woman finally spoke, her voice teary. "Oh, Bo, I choked up for a moment. I knew all along you could solve this murder, no matter how long ago it happened. Thank you, thank you, thank you!"

"No problem, Agatha. If you have any other crimes you want solved, it would be my pleasure." He said good-bye and hung up.

He called Daisy back into his office. "Pugh say anything to you about Kincaid before he left?"

She sat down across the desk from him. "No, was he supposed to?"

"Nope, I just thought he might have mentioned something to you. I'm just afraid . . ."

"He's been pretty busy, Bo. He hasn't come into the office for nearly a week. I know he was very upset over what that monster did to the old couple. Maybe Kincaid has given up trying to . . ."

She stared out the window behind Tully. He saw her eyes widen in either fear or horror.

"What's wrong?" he asked.

Suddenly, Daisy came flying over his desk. He held up his hands to fend her off but was too late. His chair went over backward. Glass shattered. A rifle shot rang in his ears. Something hit him hard in the back of the head and he blacked out. He was engulfed in darkness. So this is what it feels like to be shot in the back of the head! He didn't see a tunnel of light. This could be bad. Then

256

he opened his eyes. Daisy was sitting astraddle of him, her face pressed against his. Pieces of glass were falling out of the window. His head hurt. Daisy was crying. "Bo! Bo! Bo! Are you hit?" She was kissing his face all over, smearing it with her tears. "Don't die, Bo!" she cried. "Don't die! Don't die! I love you so much!"

Then Herb was hovering over them. He lifted Daisy to her feet. "That was close, Bo," he said. "He nearly had you."

Daisy ran back to her desk, threw herself into her chair, and put her face down on her arms.

Tully felt the back of his head for blood. It was dry. For that much pain, he was disappointed to see no blood on his hand. He deserved a little blood.

"Daisy saved your life, Bo," Herb said. "There's the bullet hole in the gun cabinet."

"Something hit me in the head," Tully said.

"Your head smacked the windowsill when you went over. That bullet missed the two of you by a good half inch."

Herb took Tully's hand and pulled him up. "The shooter is still out there in his boat, trying to get his outboard started."

Tully looked out the window. A man was standing up in the stern of the boat, flailing away at his starter cord. A sheriff's department's launch was bearing down on him. A deputy stood in the open bow of the launch, a shotgun at his shoulder. The shooter raised his hands.

"Can you see if it's Kincaid?" Tully asked.

"Not from this distance," Herb said. "It probably is though."

"It's not Kincaid," Brian Pugh said from the doorway. "It must be one of your other disgruntled criminals, Bo."

"Brian!" Tully jumped up and hugged the startled deputy. Then he shoved him away, still holding him by the shoulders. "Where on earth have you been?"

"I decided to take a few days off and get my head clear. I went up to Worley and got a room at the Coeur d'Alene Casino Hotel."

"You've been gambling."

"Not as big a gamble as tracking Kincaid."

Tully turned his chair upright and flopped down into it. He glanced at Daisy. She still had her head down on her arms. Her shoulders were shaking.

Tully said, "Herb, I've got to see Pugh alone for a minute. Go look after Daisy, will you?"

Herb left. Pugh shut the door. He walked over and examined the small round hole in the gun cabinet. "Heck of a shot," he said.

"That far away and from a boat." He pulled up Daisy's chair and sat down across from Tully. He set a plastic sack on the desk.

"You sure the guy out there isn't Kincaid?" Tully asked the deputy.

"I'm sure. You were right about the ridge on Deadman."

"Kincaid got off a shot and nearly hit me. I was surprised he missed."

"He didn't get off a shot."

"He didn't?"

"No. The shot you heard on Deadman wasn't Kincaid's. It was mine. Like you told me, I found a good spot overlooking the ridge two days before. Nothing the first day. I watched it until dark and afterward in the moonlight. Still no Kincaid. Sometime around midnight I must have dozed off. Suddenly I woke up. It was almost sunrise. I looked down and there was Kincaid, sitting cross-legged at the edge of the ridge, a rifle across his knees, still as a stone Buddha. I put him in the crosshairs. Just as the sun came up, you must have stepped out of the tent, because he suddenly whipped up the rifle. I squeezed off my shot. By the way, I brought you a little trophy for your wall." He nodded at the sack.

Tully stared at it. He thought Pugh might have slipped over the edge. Probably should give him another two weeks off. He was afraid to look in the sack, wondering what grotesque trophy his deputy might have brought him. He reached over and gingerly opened the sack with two fingers. He stood up, bent over, and peeked inside.

It was a red-and-black plaid cap with earmuffs tied up on top.

Relieved, Tully sat back down.

"It was a nasty business," Pugh said. "After I got the body disposed of, I took off all my clothes and buried them. Then I washed in the creek and put on some dry clothes. When I got in the tub at the hotel I ran it full of hot water half a dozen times before I figured I'd got the smell of Kincaid off me. Now he's got a permanent resting place up on the mountain. Nobody will ever find him."

"Old Lucas would like that."

"Who cares?" Pugh got up and headed for the door.

"One more thing, Brian. How much did you lose at the casino?"

"Nothing, Bo. I won a hundred and fifty dollars. The county lost about four hundred, though."

"A small price to pay."

Tully walked out to check on Daisy. She was sitting up now, her elbows on her desk

260

and her head in her hands. "You just saved my life," he said.

"I feel so stupid!" she said. "Stupid! Stupid! Stupid!"

"For saving my life?"

"You know what I mean."

"I think we both could use a good stiff drink. How about it, Daisy?"

"Sounds good to me," she said. "What about the office?"

"We'll let Flo handle it."

Tully got home at nearly midnight. For once in a long while, he didn't bother to scan the ridge, even in the bright moonlight. He turned his key in the lock and went in. He was pretty sure his house would no longer feel empty. When even a miserable little beast like Clarence becomes company, you know you're in trouble. Now, Tully thought, he would be okay. Sometimes just okay feels pretty darn good.

"What happened to the big painting of Ginger?" Daisy said, closing the door behind them. "I love that painting."

"I do, too," Tully said. "And tomorrow I'm going to get it back."

ABOUT THE AUTHOR

Patrick F. McManus is a renowned outdoor writer and humorist and was a longtime columnist for *Outdoor Life* and *Field & Stream.* He is the author of many books, including such runaway *New York Times* bestsellers as *The Grasshopper Trap, The Night the Bear Ate Goombaw,* and *Real Ponies Don't Go Oink!* He lives in Spokane, Washington. Visit him online at www .patrickfmcmanus.com.

The employees of Thorndike Press hope you have enjoyed this Large Print book. All our Thorndike, Wheeler, and Kennebec Large Print titles are designed for easy reading, and all our books are made to last. Other Thorndike Press Large Print books are available at your library, through selected bookstores, or directly from us.

For information about titles, please call:
(800) 223-1244

or visit our Web site at:
http://gale.cengage.com/thorndike

To share your comments, please write:
Publisher
Thorndike Press
295 Kennedy Memorial Drive
Waterville, ME 04901